No Time for Ribbons

A Novel

by

Craig Trebilcock

iUniverse, Inc.
New York   Bloomington

No Time for Ribbons
A Novel

This is a work of fiction. All of the characters, names, incidents, organizations, and dialogue in this novel are either the products of the author's imagination or are used fictitiously. This story, while based upon the wartime and postwar experiences of soldiers and marines who served in the Iraq War, has fictitious elements interjected to preserve story cohesion. This book is written in the author's civilian capacity and in no way represents or reflects the views of the US Army or Department of Defense.

iUniverse books may be ordered through booksellers or by contacting:

iUniverse
1663 Liberty Drive
Bloomington, IN 47403
www.iuniverse.com
1-800-Authors (1-800-288-4677)

ISBN: 978-0-595-49286-2 (pbk)
ISBN: 978-0-595-50867-9 (cloth)
ISBN: 978-0-595-61043-3 (ebk)

Printed in the United States of America

Also by Craig Trebilcock

One Weekend A Month

For Terrie, Aubrey, and Joseph, who also served.

"People sleep peaceably in their beds at night only because rough men stand ready to do violence on their behalf."

- Eric Arthur Blair (George Orwell)

ACKNOWLEDGMENTS

This book is possible due to the outstanding editing support from Ms. Kathy Rogers, a lady of gentile manner and intelligence, whose red pen contributed greatly to this story. Thanks also to my technical advisor, The Evil Twin, who helped keep a JAG officer in his lane when describing military ceremonies, awards, and weapons systems.

Preface

I knew that I was home the day the old lady with the "JESUS" plate on her station wagon gave me the finger at a stoplight.

Our brigade returned after four months' training to go to war, a year on the ground in Iraq and Kuwait, and three days' postwar screening to ensure that we weren't a danger to society. That we'd been conditioned during the prior sixteen months to inflict maximum violence on someone else's society was politely overlooked.

We had our arms shot full of goo that the docs claimed would immunize us from the exotic Middle Eastern germs lurking in the desert – it didn't. We'd been conditioned to kill, to hand out teddy bears, and to tell friendly fire from hostile just by the report of the weapon several blocks away. We'd been told that we were going to destroy the Iraqi army, and then when that reality was no longer convenient, instructed we were there to rebuild it.

We muttered "bullshit" when the order came down to not fly the American flag in Iraq as it might offend the indigenous population when the suits in DC didn't want to be viewed as conquerors: nearly two thousand dead Iraqi tanks testified otherwise. We'd been briefed that we weren't there to nation build and we'd be home within six months – until the suits thought we needed to save these people from three thousand years of their own social evolution by delivering a ration of Western democracy. Just add water...

The briefings at Fort Bragg before we deployed had been very comforting. We would have military police or security escorts with heavy crew-served weapons supporting our missions to win over the Iraqi civilians, as no one in their right mind expected lightly trained reservists from a non-combat arms branch to make their own way through a hostile desert in the middle of a war. I remembered this helpful information weeks later as I stood over a map spread across the hood of my HMMWV, lost, as I cut a path through the Iraqi desert without security escort, in the middle of the war.

That was the first hint that there wouldn't be a noncompetitive category in this game. It was either get smart quick or get dead quicker. We got smart, stopped believing the convenient truths ladled out to us, and kept each other alive. In the process we changed and so did our view of the world.

Returning home, we left a broken society behind where bad luck, bad people, and bad living had been the norm for three thousand years, to reenter a culture where a lukewarm latte was enough to reduce many to quivering cries of outrage; where people *really* cared who won a contrived TV talent show; where the dead from our "war for the nation's survival" were already relegated to page seventeen. *Had it been like this before?*

The first challenge in the homecoming was that the things that make you a really good soldier often make you a really bad civilian. Constant vigilance to external threats, hair-trigger reactions to unexpected sound or movement, and eyes in the back of your head were necessary for survival in Iraq, where the civilians and the bad guys were identical in appearance – right until the moment they tried to kill you. The problem is that when you bring those skills home, you're not the funniest guy at neighborhood parties anymore. The T-shirt I saw at Fort Bragg captured the mentality: "Be nice to everyone you meet, but have a plan to kill them if necessary."

The second problem was that no one told us that going to war was the easy part. Years of military discipline and training had prepared us for that. We had no training on how to turn it off afterwards. Coming home to peace was to be the real bitch.

The final challenge was reconciling our accounts from the war with a nation that chooses not to recognize it is at war. A very small number of volunteers keep the barbarians from the gates these days. The shared sacrifice of national defense belongs to another period in our history.

As a society we like our heroes stoic and humble. We revel in the story of the unsung young man from Paducah who seizes the enemy position without regard to personal danger. We are not quite so comfortable hearing about the guilt the young man bears – or how the emotional armor he girded to survive the savagery of war now keeps old friends and family at arm's length. It intrudes upon our hero fantasy and uncomfortably reminds us that even the stalwart among us are breakable.

Like its predecessor, <u>One Weekend A Month</u>, this volume presents a window into our society's ongoing "War on Terror." This is the unseen story of the home front – the conflict that burns inside our men and women after we bring them home from foreign battlefields and burden them with the label "hero." It is a tale built upon the actual postwar experience of the office workers, policemen, and students who marched off in the first decade of the millennium to protect the realm. In many ways this is a more unsettling war than the one fought overseas with weapons, as it occurs every day, in our homes and towns, without end.

This book is written in tribute to those whose vigil at the frontier molds and forever separates them from the very society they fight to preserve.

U.S. Army Enlisted Rank

U.S. Army Officer Rank

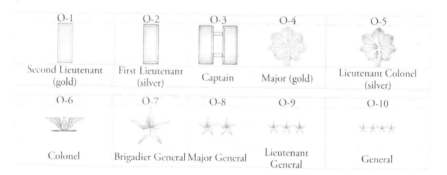

CIVIL AFFAIRS COMMAND STRUCTURE

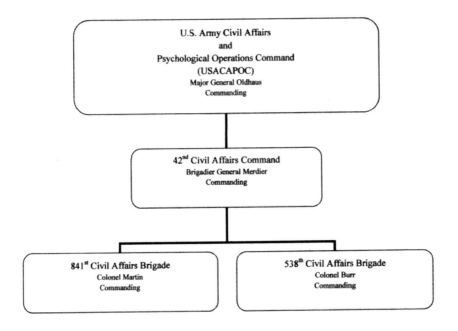

Vignette

On the April morning that the convoy rolled northward toward Baghdad, the Lieutenant saw the old man in the red checkered keffiyah sitting on the Euphrates River bridge. The wizened figure sat along the curb – his thin, sun-baked arms turned upward at the elbows, palms raised toward heaven. "God Bless the United States of America," he intoned reverently in thick English, as the Lieutenant's HMMWV chugged past. Tears streaked the old man's cheeks, welling from thankful eyes set in a deeply lined face. It was a moment that burned itself forever into the young officer's memory. *We have made a difference here,* he recognized with satisfaction.

The fighting had passed through Nasiriyah only days before, leaving many buildings still smoldering from the determined fight. The Iraqi Army had shown uncharacteristic resolve in holding these bridges against the advancing Marines, inflicting substantial casualties before withdrawing. Moving up in the wake of that bitter fighting, the

Lieutenant had not been sure what his small convoy would encounter when entering the town.

The smiles from the people took him off guard. Children skipped beside the slow-moving convoy, happily offering the sale of worthless Saddam currency in high, piping voices. Merchants cheerfully hawked fresh produce from overflowing tables, belying the news stories of deprivation in the days prior to the invasion. Young women shyly smiled at the young Americans. *These are not enemies,* the Lieutenant thought. A holiday atmosphere mocked the soldier's attempt at martial solemnity.

A year passed, and the next rotation of those who would save the people came. The Lieutenant and what was left of his platoon no longer cared to save the world. Gaunt, wolfish features had replaced the full, hopeful faces of 2003. Ragged, salt-stained uniforms hung from lean frames. Weary hands held weapons close.

The limping vehicles left tracks of oil behind them as they moved south through Nasiriyah. Memories of the prior spring had faded. No one thanked them. Women averted their eyes. Children no longer pursued them with glee.

The Lieutenant signaled the convoy to stop before crossing the river. He climbed into the roof gunner's position and surveyed the bridge's length, seeing only an old man sitting on the near curb staring into the gutter. His tattered, red and white checkered keffiyah hung limply over slumped shoulders. The Lieutenant measured at a glance that he was not a threat.

The Lieutenant directed his HMMWV onto the bridge. As the vehicle came even with the old man, dull, deep-set eyes rose to survey the vehicle. The old man pursed his lips and directed a stream of brown spittle at its tires. "Infidel," he whispered.

Haji bastard, glared the Lieutenant's eyes, before turning again toward the promise of Kuwait and home.

Chapter 1
The Sprinter

Outskirts of Baghdad – 27 March 2004

"Jaguar Two, this is Jaguar One, over."

No answer.

"Jaguar Two, do you read?" repeated Sergeant First Class Gus Warden into his handset.

Again, no response.

A year in the heat and dust of Iraq had taken a toll on the equipment and personnel of Team Jaguar, the eight-man government reconstruction team of the 538th Civil Affairs Brigade. Radios functioned at their whim, the vehicles were in the maintenance shop more than on the road, and the lean veterans of America's war in Iraq had become accustomed to operating without luxuries such as working equipment.

The 538ᵗʰ CA Brigade was one of the many Army Reserve units called up from across America for the initial invasion of Iraq in March 2003. Its 144 part-time soldiers were trained to run a small country if need be during times of natural disaster or military occupation. Engineers, doctors, lawyers, and civil administrators comprised the unit, which was seemingly tailor-made for trying to piece Iraq back together again.

Today's mission was the end of a long journey for the Jaguars. Having said farewell to their wounded officer-in-charge (OIC), Major Bill Trevanathan, the day before, the remainder of the team was completing the final mission of their year-long deployment: escorting their brigade commander, Colonel Richard Hermann to the heavily defended Green Zone in Baghdad. There Colonel Hermann would officially hand over responsibility for the 538ᵗʰ's mission to the incoming 803ʳᵈ Civil Affairs Brigade. Tomorrow they would all be on a chartered 747 flight out of the former Saddam International Airport back to Fort Bragg, North Carolina, and finally home.

Major Trevanathan – "Major T" as the team called him due to his lengthy name – had been severely wounded by a roadside bomb the week before near their base of operations at Camp Babylon. The attack had killed their Kuwaiti translator, Abu, and left Major T with a baseball-sized hole in his abdomen. The rest of the team was still unnerved, after previously embracing the overly optimistic belief that they had made it safely to the end of their tour.

We're not going to repeat that cluster today, thought Warden as he twisted in the front passenger seat of his HMMWV to see why the following vehicle, Jaguar Two, was not responding to his radio calls. Looking past the brigade commander seated immediately behind him, Warden could see Captain Rick Smith, the acting OIC of their team, sitting behind the dust-smeared windshield of Jaguar Two. Warden held the handset to the radio out the side of his vehicle, rotating it in the air to catch Smith's attention.

In reply, Smith held his own handset out and made a thumbs-down signal with his left hand. *Gotta' love low-bidder contracting,* thought Warden. *We're on one of the most dangerous roads in the world and I can't talk to my other team fifty yards away. Guess the Pentagon never 'magined we might go to war someplace dirty and hot.*

Warden turned to face forward again, seeing that they were approaching a stretch of road that ran past a makeshift roadside market. A long line of civilian tractor trailers sat nose to tail twenty feet off the right side of the main road. Behind this man-made wall a makeshift collection of tables were assembled where the locals bartered everything from truck parts to vegetables. Warden looked over at the driver's dash to make sure that they were keeping up a good speed. *Only defense against an IED[1] in these canvas coffins is makin' it miss ya',* he thought, satisfied with their pace.

Focusing his attention now upon the Iraqi civilians carrying out their business on the far side of the approaching trucks, Warden resolved, *If I never see one of these people again, it'll be fine with me.* With an experienced eye he quickly assessed the Iraqis for any sign of a threat. Warden had lost a close friend to a sniper in the abortive

7

relief mission in Somalia several years before and had nearly lost this civil affairs team in the roadside ambush a week before. Warden had had his fill of the Islamic world and the politicians' dead end attempts to 'democratize' Iraq. Not one sensitive to the boundaries of political correctness, his favorite shorthand reference to Iraqis as "terrorists" was liberally applied to civilians and combatants alike.

Looks normal; no lookouts, no one seeking cover, no apparent signals. Damn, I wish I could get the Captain on the radio, though – those trucks parked so close to the highway are bad news. Could be anything in those and we'd never know what hit us, Warden weighed soberly.

Warden had been in the rear seat of the old Jaguar One when a Soviet-made 122 mm artillery shell wired to a guardrail by insurgents had destroyed that vehicle. The tremendous blast had splattered him with most of their translator's face; Abu had unluckily caught the full brunt of the explosion on his side of the vehicle. Warden had been experiencing bouts of blurred vision and headaches ever since, but wasn't reporting that to anyone until he was back home in Texas. *Not going to give the Army any more excuses to keep me from my family,* he thought bitterly. *I mention this, and they'll slap me into a sick ward in Germany for months while everyone else goes home.* The 538th had already been extended twice during its tour, and the level of trust between the Reservists and the Army was now almost nonexistent.

"Cooper, keep an eye out for anything between those trucks and the road," he instructed the Private First Class sitting to his left. The warning was unnecessary: Mark Cooper was also a survivor of the previous week's IED attack. His white knuckles on the steering wheel betrayed his absolute concentration as they entered the choke point.

They had nearly cleared the trailers when Warden turned around again to ensure that Jaguar Two was maintaining a good convoy interval. His first indication that this was not to be an uneventful mission was being thrown violently backwards, his helmet smashing against the windshield, as Cooper locked the brakes. Facing the wrong direction, Warden did not see the white Isuzu pickup truck suddenly dart out from behind the row of trailers ahead of them, cutting the convoy off. He did hear the screech of Jaguar Two's brakes close behind them, as Smith's driver, Private First Class Tyler Jamie, tried to avoid Warden's HMMWV.

The familiar, sickening feeling of the world going into slow motion washed over Warden as he heard Sergeant Tim Mantis yelling "Aammbushh!" from the rear driver's side seat. Mantis manned the squad automated weapon (SAW), the Army's current version of a light machine gun. Warden painfully turned his neck to see what had caused their sudden halt, thumbing his rifle off "safe" as he turned. Thirty feet ahead, a small white truck blocked their path, its doors open as the two Iraqis inside poured out.

Classic blocking ambush, Warden assessed as he struggled to get his large frame, burdened with a twenty-five pound flak jacket, out the open door of the HMMWV. *Cut off the lead vehicle – cause the following convoy to jam up behind – kill the entire package.* He righted himself heavily and forced his legs out the passenger side. His head still rang, and tears streamed from the corners of his eyes from the impact.

As his feet made contact with the pavement, sudden movement toward the rear of the convoy caught Warden's eye. An insurgent wearing a blue, ankle-length dishdash "man dress," burst from a gap between two trailers, running directly at Warden. *Hitting us from front and rear,* Warden instinctively recognized. In the HMMWV's back seat, Colonel Hermann fumbled to free himself from his seat belt, distracting Warden for an instant. Directing his blurred vision back toward the sprinter, Warden sensed…*something in his hand…detonator?* Without further hesitation Warden brought his weapon to his shoulder and squeezed the trigger.

CRACK!

The target's legs ran three more steps after the round hit before collapsing. Warden's 5.56mm bullet had penetrated the Iraqi's sternum and tumbled through his chest cavity, shattering the spinal column and blowing a sizable hole between his shoulder blades as it exited. With a shocked expression, the target crumpled onto his back as Warden whirled and dropped to one knee to engage the threat from the pickup.

The two Iraqis from the pickup were standing side by side, hands in the air, as Cooper and Mantis cautiously approached them with raised weapons. The older of the two wore a white dishdash and a small skull cap. The other, in his early twenties, wore blue jeans and a stained Coca-Cola T-shirt. Wiping his eyes clear, Warden saw no apparent threat from either of them and turned his attention to the rear of the convoy. *Nothing.* He glanced beneath the belly of trailer for moving legs on the far side. *Nothing.* Warden's heart pounded inside his flak jacket and he gulped for air against the confines of his flak jacket. His senses were on overdrive as he searched for any hostile movement. "You're never quite so alive as when someone's trying to kill you," his friend Pete Leader had told him many times.

Warden saw that Captain Smith and Staff Sergeant Leader had dismounted from Jaguar Two. Smith turned and reached back into the vehicle while Leader cautiously approached the downed attacker. Leader held his M16 at the ready, diagonally across his waist. "Be careful, Pete, I think he's wired," Warden warned. Leader nodded.

"Mantis - search and zip cuff those two Hajis," Warden ordered over his shoulder as he stood and moved to join Leader. Down the length of the four-vehicle convoy the remainder of the troops belatedly unfolded themselves from their HMMWVs, assuming security positions beside their idling vehicles.

Warden kept an eye on the gaps between the trailers as he walked. *Damn it – they can come jumping out from between any of them,* he evaluated, *and we can't see 'em coming.* He quickly kneeled again, looking for any activity beneath or behind the trailers. *Nothing.* Walking the remaining distance to Leader he thought, *This is damn funny that they'd attack with only three – maybe they're waiting until we bunch up? Maybe one of these trailers is packed with explosives?* He looked for any signs that might reveal such a trap. His mind whirled with a year's worth of survival experience, trying to make combat sense of their situation.

Leader was standing over the body as Warden walked up. A small round hole was perfectly centered in the target's chest; a pool of blood seeped out from under the dead insurgent, framing the body. "Nice shot," Leader offered without emotion.

"Yeah, helluva' thing on our last day, huh?" Warden replied, gazing at the corpse with the cold professional detachment that comes from war. Flies were already crawling across the stain on his chest. Several had landed on the face as well, leaving small bloody flecks on the dusky cheeks. Warden did another quick 360-degree scan for the follow-on attack. *This makes no sense. C'mon! Hit us, damnit!*

Leader knelt next to the dead insurgent, whose left arm ended in a closed fist. With just his eyes, Leader carefully examined the arm, searching for the wire leading to charges likely concealed beneath the man's clothing. He pulled a small knife from his pocket - bought at the makeshift market outside the gate at Camp Babylon - and flipped open the blade. Gently, he probed between the man's side and outstretched arm, seeking the slightest resistance that might reveal the detonation wire.

"I'm gettin' nuthin'," he said without looking up.

"Could be a remote," warned Warden, silently cursing the impaired vision that rendered him useless for this detailed task.

"Mebbe'," replied Leader. He laid the knife down next to the body before cautiously reaching over with his right hand to lightly probe the abdomen for an explosive belt. Despite the delicacy of his task, the muscles of his massive arms were taut with tension.

"Waddya' have?" asked Captain Smith as he walked up. "The Old Man wants a report. I don't want him over here until we're sure what we have."

Leader looked toward the pickup, where he could see the brigade commander interrogating one of the two Iraqis along the roadside.

"Seems like we have a Haji havin' a bad day here, sir," replied Leader, returning his attention to the man's closed fist. Leader gently reached his fingers beneath the insurgent's hand and lifted it.

"Pete…" Warden warned.

As Leader elevated the lifeless hand its fingers loosened and fell open, spilling a string of tiny wooden spheres onto the ground.

"Prayer beads," breathed Smith.

Warden said nothing, trying hard to focus on the object that was used ritualistically by Iraqis during their daily devotions. It was still a blur to him.

"Holy shit!" Smith blurted. "We killed a guy with a handful of prayer beads."

"No sir," interrupted Leader emphatically. "No… sir," he repeated, shaking his head and drawing out his words for emphasis. "This here Haji was charging at the vehicle containing our brigade commander with a weapon. Sergeant Warden shot him in self defense. It's as clear as day." Leader picked up the four-inch knife and hefted it in his hand. He turned his head to look straight into Smith's face. "He had a weapon, sir."

Smith said nothing, meeting Leader's steady gaze.

"Captain Smith…Captain Smith, what is the situation?" the brigade commander called from the front of the convoy. "Traffic is piling up pretty good behind us."

Smith looked to the rear of their small convoy, where two of his troops were motioning for a group of increasingly animated Iraqi motorists to stay back from the scene.

"Sergeant Warden?" Smith asked, turning his attention to the broad shouldered NCO. "Is that what happened?" he asked in a slightly shaky voice. Smith had been an enlisted man in the first Gulf War and was no stranger to casualties. The adrenalin was beginning to wear off of all of them now, however, leaving behind the slightly nauseous feeling that follows a firefight.

"I,…I gotta' be honest, Sir," Warden stammered, pain pounding at his temples from the blow to his head. "I saw this Haji runnin' at the brigade commander's vehicle after we got cut off, and I saw he had somethin' in his hand…"

"…which was a knife and some Haji 'take me to Allah beads'" insisted Leader, standing slowly. "Because you know what? This guy is just as dead either way." Leader dropped the knife into the slurry of blood and dirt next to the body. "Sir, I've seen things like this back on the beat in Baltimore," he advised. "If we don't square this crap away *right now* and make it tight, there's gonna' be months of investigations, and nobody's goin' home."

"So I'm supposed to tell the Colonel this guy was attacking our convoy with a *knife*, Sergeant Leader?" Smith asked doubtfully.

"Sir, there's no accounting for what these crazy Haji bastards are gonna' do," Leader insisted. "Seems like it was probably just a spur of the moment thing – not planned or nuthin.' Mebbe' the sun got to him. Mebbe' some other troop shot one of his relatives yesterday. Who knows? We can't be expected to explain these people's actions."

Smith shook his head, unconvinced. "Nobody's gonna' believe that," he said dismally, averting his eyes to avoid the accusing look on the dead man's face. Noticing a glint of metal from the corpse's other closed fist, Smith ordered, "Check his other hand. But be careful."

Leader moved around the body and scrutinized its right hand before carefully opening the fingers. A large key on a leather tag fell from the palm. Leader picked it up and read the tag. "Volvo," he said. "Looks like he's one of the truck drivers."

"Captain Smith!" demanded Colonel Hermann as he approached the group. "I asked you for a sitrep!²" Without pausing for a reply, Colonel Hermann added, "Seems the truck up front was just lousy Iraqi driving. No weapons. Both men work out at the airport – they check out clean." The brigade commander stopped speaking as his eyes fell upon the body. "What's this?"

"Sir," announced Sergeant Leader before Smith could speak. "This Haji tried to take advantage of the confusion from the pickup jammin' up our convoy to sneak up on your vehicle with a weapon. Sergeant Warden took him out."

"Really?" asked the Colonel to no one in particular, a look of surprise on his long features. "That's incredible…" He stared silently down at the dead man for several seconds. Colonel Hermann's eyes moved to the open knife. "How did you spot him, Sergeant Warden?" the brigade commander inquired absently, mesmerized by the spreading pool of blood.

Warden saw the warning in Pete Leader's eyes as he replied. "I just rolled out of the vehicle and he was comin' at me, Sir. I just reacted."

Even after a year deployed with the man, Hermann's gentile Yankee ear had a hard time understanding Warden's exaggerated Texas drawl. The man's "I" sounded like "Ahh" and his "Sir" sounded like "Sahr." Sometimes he wondered if the Texan wasn't just having him on, but Hermann lacked the confidence to ever raise such a thought. Warden was one of the few prior combat veterans in the unit and exuded a steely resolve that signaled he was not interested in idle chatter with officers.

No one spoke, waiting for the commander's reaction – a reaction that would mean the difference between their going home tomorrow or months of bureaucratic investigation while they rotted on a desert base camp somewhere.

Raising his gaze away from the dead man, Hermann ordered, "Well, let's mount up – the General is waiting for us."

"Sir?" gulped Captain Smith. "What about the body?"

"Well,…we're already running late – just have the two Hajis with the pickup truck throw it in back and haul it to the nearest police station. Sergeant Leader, help them load it up. *Nothing* is going to keep us from that flight tomorrow. Let's move!"

Chapter 2
The Oasis

Fort Bragg, North Carolina – 2 April 2004

"This train is leavin' in five minutes, y'all," declared Warden as he looked about the second floor bay of the old wooden barracks. The Jaguar team's wartime deployment had come full circle. After a year in the desert, they now found themselves back in the same whitewashed, ramshackle WWII barracks in the old division area from which they had mobilized to Iraq.

A year had not improved the Spartan quarters, whose amenities were limited to 1940s era plumbing, sporadic heating, and no air conditioning. The same two rows of metal framed bunks with their saggy springs and stained mattresses greeted the team when they debarked from the bus from neighboring Pope Air Force Base.

What *had* changed in the past year, however, were the expectations of the team, who greeted their formerly despised, barren quarters with enthusiasm. Indoor latrines, windows with glass, and a view that included green pine trees were total luxuries; complaints from the prior spring about the absence of hot water and cheap government toilet paper were gone. Having learned to be scavengers in the desert, the only complaint came from the housekeeping staff, as the men kept stealing the precious rolls of tissue to hide in their rucksacks.

Warden and Leader chose bunks at the top of the second floor stairs, which had been designated as enlisted billeting. The company grade officers, including Captain Smith, were on the first floor below them. The gaggle of "light" and full colonels comprising nearly a third of the unit was in a separate barracks next door, segregated for their own peace of mind. As they had done in the desert, the six enlisted and NCO members of team Jaguar had chosen sleeping areas in close proximity to one another, even though the spacious second floor was mostly empty on account of the large number of 538th personnel who had returned early from the deployment due to personal emergencies, real or contrived.

The team had joked and dreamed of their return to the pleasures of American life every day for the past twelve months. Tonight was their first step in re-acclimating to that society. After a couple days of badly needed sleep, showers, and some mandatory psychiatric screenings to ensure no lingering issues were about to be let loose on the citizens of Fayetteville, the Jaguars were about to enjoy their first night out of uniform in a year.

The rules of the demobilization command under which they now fell for two weeks of out-processing specified that no one below the rank of major was authorized to rent a car on post. To men who had just served a year in the desert, facing every conceivable danger and discomfort, such rear-echelon prohibitions were not taken seriously. Leader had returned to the barracks on their second day at Bragg driving a cherry-red Chevy convertible that had immediately been dubbed "Jaguar One" by the team. Sergeant Warden, who was responsible for the conduct of the team during their demobilization, had just smiled and turned the other way as Leader roared into the company area behind the wheel of the contraband vehicle.

"Time, tide, and margaritas wait for no man," Warden declared to his men with a rare smile. "Hey, where's Leader?" he asked to the room in general, noticing that the second ranking NCO of the Jaguar team wasn't present.

"He's still over at the CIF³ turning in his shit, Sergeant," replied Specialist Cooper, the quiet and slightly bookish member of Team Jaguar, employing field slang for one's basic issue of equipment. Cooper was enjoying not only his return home, but also his promotion from Private First Class the day before.

As if on cue, the door at the base of the stairwell slammed with a jarring impact as Pete Leader's familiar bellow ricocheted up the stairwell. "Damn it!" he roared, stomping up the stairs. "I've never seen such a rat screw in all my life!"

Warden hung his head and shook it slightly with an amused smile on his lips. *Guess we won't be leaving in five minutes after all,* he thought.

Leader burst into the open bay of the barracks. "Shit!" he added for emphasis, upon the small chance that there was anyone within a hundred meters who was not yet aware he was angry. He threw his empty duffel bag onto his bunk with vehemence.

"Rough day at the office, hon?" Warden baited Leader, knowing the inquiry would likely trigger another spasm of profanity.

"Goddamn right! Now listen to this," Leader declared, sitting down on the bunk as he bent to unlace his sand colored boots. "I get to CIF and start turning in my gear. I knew I was gonna' get gigged for a couple small items. I shit-canned that shelter-half as soon as we moved into Iraq, and Dale Earnhardt here drove over my goggles at Camp Commando," he gestured with his thumb at Private First Class Ridlin, who sat happily on his own bunk with his ever vacuous look on his face. "So I knew I was gonna' hafta' pay about a hundred bucks to those vultures at CIF."

Warden patiently listened as Leader began working on his other boot.

"So I get all the way to the last turn-in station with no problem, right?" he asked rhetorically, "Until I get to this crotchety old fossil – 'bout three hundred years old – at the last counter. I turn in my flak jacket to him, and he says in that bored CIF voice, 'This isn't the flak jacket you were issued.'"

"You remember how Major T traded me out his jacket when we first got in country, right?" Leader asked his audience.

Warden and the rest of the team nodded soberly. Every member of the team knew that Major Trevanathan's willingness to trade Leader his larger, better-fitting flak jacket had directly contributed to their officer being wounded on their last mission. Shrapnel from the exploding enemy IED had penetrated Trevanathan's back just beneath the bottom of his too-small flak jacket. The white-hot fragment had shredded one kidney and blown a significant length of intestine out of the officer's abdomen. Only prompt emergency care from his team and an emergency helicopter evacuation to the surgical table had saved the officer's life.

The image of Trevanathan lying in the bottom of the drainage ditch mouthing "my fault" came to Warden as clearly as if he was back in that shallow culvert with enemy rounds still snapping over his head. No longer at Fort Bragg, Warden watched the color fade from his officer's face as he struggled to get pressure on the entry and exit wounds that were spilling the Major's life into the sand.

"...'Bullshit,' I told him," Leader continued, his rising volume bringing Warden back into the room. "'I signed for a flak jacket and I'm returning a flak jacket.' But this fossil says that unless I can bring back the very *same* flak jacket I have to pay for the original one – a $395 price tag. He says because there's been so much theft downrange, they made this new policy."

"Didn't ya' tell him what happened to the original one, Serg'nt?" asked Private First Class Jamie, the team's automatic weapons handler from Amarillo. "That thing was soaked with blood and crap when they med-evac'd the Major. No way anybody was ever wearin' that thing again." Jamie's round face flushed as he remembered lying in the irrigation ditch providing cover fire as Warden and Cooper struggled to stop Trevanathan's bleeding.

"Oh yeah, I told him…," said Leader as he turned and dropped his uniform pants, revealing that he had continued the field practice of "going commando" since returning to the States. Like most troops in the field, Leader avoided the civilian custom of underwear as it created "heat pockets" in hot or humid environments that led to rashes and attracted insects.

"Christ, Pete," complained Warden. "I've had to stare at that sorry ass of yours for the past year – would it be too much trouble for you to buy a pair of 'wares at the PX now that we're back in the world?"

"Flashing you is the only thing that gets me out of bed in the morning, Sergeant Warden," Leader bantered back to his friend.

Warden smirked. "You have a backside that only a Haji prison guard could love. Now why don't ya' finish your soap opera, so's we can get the hell outta' here. I haven't been in a bar for a year, and you're holdin' up progress."

Leader resumed his account, hardly losing a beat. "Jamie called it. I told this old bastard that my flak got blown up with my officer inside it. You know what he says then?" Leader paused for dramatic effect. "He asks me for a hand receipt to prove that I really traded it to Major T."

"Man…" stated Jamie to no one in particular. "Do those guys have any idea what it's like over there?"

"So now I'm standin' there and the old bastard hands me a statement of charges for the flak jacket for $395," Leader continued. "Tells me I can pay cash, or it'll be taken out of my final pay."

"So, what'd ya' do?" Warden asked, as Leader pulled on a bright blue, flowered Hawaiian shirt.

"Well, I gotta' tell ya', the temptation was pretty strong to drag that smug old fart across the counter and shake the crap outta' him," replied Leader, taking a tentative sniff at the shirt that had been rolled up in the bottom of his duffel bag for the past year. "But I knew you heroes were waiting for me, and a trip to the D-cell[4] might put a damper on this evening's festivities."

"So you paid?" Jamie asked, incredulously.

"Not exactly," replied Leader with a mischievous grin. "I took the statement of charges from him and checked off the block to have the money taken from my last paycheck. Then I shoved the paper down the back of my pants, wiped my crack with it, and handed it back."

"No damn way!" exclaimed Jamie gleefully. He rocked back on his bunk, giggling at the mental picture.

Warden shook his head and looked at Leader's big smile, knowing that every word of it was true.

Cooper buried his face in his hands, his ears and neck turning bright red as he quietly sniggered. Even Mantis, who had never had even a slightly positive relationship with Leader, grinned from ear to ear. The thought of someone striking back at the cattle-call, impersonal bureaucracy of the mobilization station functionaries impressed even him.

"He just 'bout fell off his stool behind the counter," Leader concluded, lacing up a pair of suede Hush Puppies. "I just turned and left as he started screaming, 'You get back here, sergeant!' I'm pretty sure that's one statement of charges they won't be processing."

Unable to suppress his grin, Warden looked around the room at the gleeful reactions of his team. He knew they had a year's worth of frustration pent up inside them. It had been a year of nonsensical Army bureaucracy and inefficiency mixed with the daily indiscriminate violence in Iraq. Tonight's venture off post was the beginning of trying to gradually release some of that steam. He knew his own nerves had been ragged for weeks now, what with the IED ambush and his own shooting of the Haji at the truck stop. Leader's reaction to the CIF clerk was a sign of how badly that release of steam needed to be controlled. Leader was a jokester, but he was also a professional NCO who would have never acted the way he did tonight prior to their deployment. *And I wouldn't have thought it was funny either,* he inwardly rebuked himself.

Warden recalled the instructions that he had been given by their Sergeant Major an hour earlier. "Sergeant Warden, let the men blow off the pressure and have a good time, but keep a rein on things. Nobody's had a drink in nearly a year, and the combination of booze and getting out into the world again for the first time is a potent combination."

Repeating the Sergeant Major's last admonition to his men as the laughter died down, Warden issued the evening's safety briefing. "Alright, listen up: Cooper volunteered to drive tonight, so he stays dry. The rest of you are big boys and can pace yourselves. Remember you might be lightweights due to the lack of booze in theater, so take it easy. We all stay together and no fights. Any problems from any of you heroes, and we come back here and clean the barracks all night. Got it?"

"Yes, Sergn't," replied the group instinctively, used to a year's worth of safety and convoy briefings under much more serious circumstances.

"One other thing," Warden instructed. "Y'all may not have noticed, but a year in the sand has not done a whole heap to improve your vocabulary. We're goin' out among civilians who don't typically use 'Goddamn, shit, and MF' every other word to color their conversation."

"No shit?" asked Leader, drawing a smattering of laughter.

Warden fixed his friend with a stare that signaled *knock it off.*

"Sorry, mom," Leader said, sitting down with an unapologetic grin.

"So use tonight as practice for when y'all get home, so ya' don't peel the paint off the walls with your language. Everyone knows everyone 'round Bragg, and we don't need some officer's wife getting her panties in a knot 'cause one of ya' lets fly in public. Got it?"

"Yes, Sergn't," repeated the team automatically.

"All right, let's go take this town apart," declared Warden, as he headed for the door, followed by the collective war whoops of Team Jaguar.

"Good evening, my name is Bethany, and I'll be your server this evening," volunteered the perky young waitress. The table conversation instantly stopped as her bright smile captured the team's attention. She wore a yellow polo shirt and a pair of form-fitting khakis that appeared to be the uniform at "El Mexicana Grille."

"Darlin', you can do whatever you want," replied Jamie, a big smile breaking across his face as he admired their server. During the past year female company had been far from the minds of most of the team. Fatigue, a coat of grime, and a complete lack of privacy made such liaisons unlikely, even had the opportunity presented itself. The local Iraqis were clearly out of bounds both from a practical and policy basis, and most of the female troops on Camp Babylon had, like their male counterparts, been focused on survival and their mission, not romance.

"Take it easy, Lady's Man," teased Leader. Jamie grinned back good-naturedly.

"Ya'll have to bear with us, ma'am," explained Warden in his slow Texas drawl. "We just got back from overseas and some of us," he nodded his head toward the still smiling Jamie, "are a tad enthusiastic to be back in civilized company."

"Really? Where were you at?" the waitress asked. Fayetteville was a military town from top to bottom. With the presence of the 82nd Airborne Division and a variety of other Special Operations units stationed at Fort Bragg and Pope Air Force base, the locals were familiar with the frequent comings and goings of their military neighbors.

"Iraq," replied Warden. "Twelve months." The team nodded quietly in agreement.

"Welcome home to all of you," she smiled, "and thank you for your service. Twelve months? That's a long time, isn't it?"

"About eleven months too long," joked Leader to appreciative laughter from the others. The anger that they had felt after two tour extensions caused by the lack of proper planning in Washington had no place at the table tonight.

"Well, you've had a long time to build up a thirst," she teased. "What can I get for you to start?"

"I'd like a big-ass pitcher of margaritas," blurted Mantis, looking up from the colorful display of drinks on the menu before him.

"Watch your language, dumb shit," corrected Leader. "Remember what the Sergeant Major said."

"Sorry, ma'am," Mantis corrected himself, flushing slightly.

"Let's get two pitchers to start," Warden added. "Cooper, waddya' want?"

"I'd like a Coke, ma'am," Cooper replied quietly. After a pause he added hopefully, "Do you happen to have a Cherry Coke?"

"We have Cherry Coke, Lime Coke, and Vanilla Coke. Also Coke Zero."

Cooper blinked and hesitated: having choices was not something he was used to in Iraq. "Umm…, when did they come out with all of those?" he asked uncertainly.

"Oh they've been out for a long time," she replied pleasantly, waiting.

"Too many choices for me, ma'am" Cooper stammered, embarrassed. "I'll just take Cherry Coke, I guess. Thanks."

"Alrighty, I'll have those out to you in a jiffy." Bethany smiled as she turned away toward the kitchen. Six sets of eyes followed her lithe form before Jamie broke the silence with "Did you see that? She had a full set of teeth!" he admired, followed by a deep and contrived moan of attraction.

"She was pretty," added Ridlin.

"Really, Andy Hardy? Mebbe' we could put on a show together?" Leader replied to Ridlin's typical overly-obvious statement.

"Ya' know, and I know this is gonna' sound stupid," Mantis volunteered, looking in fascination at the ice cubes floating in his water glass. "I never really looked much at a woman's eyes before. Always seemed to be somethin' more interesting to focus on, ya' know? But with the Haji women all wrapped up the way they were, I really came to 'preciate how they made their eyes attractive."

"Mantis, that's the smartest dumb thing I've ever heard you say," retorted Leader. Leader and Mantis had been at each other since day one of their deployment. Mantis had been promoted to Sergeant just days before the unit flew to Iraq and Leader had little confidence in his leadership abilities. Throughout the combat tour Leader had called him a 'senior specialist,' even though Mantis had the rank of a noncommissioned officer, because Mantis possessed no experience leading and motivating troops. Mantis' early attempts during the deployment at substituting bullying for leadership had drawn constant criticism from Leader, who outranked Mantis by one pay grade and about seven years' experience.

"I'll take that as a compliment, I suppose," retorted Mantis good-naturedly. He had become somewhat immune to Leader's peculiar sense of humor over the very long year.

"No, I'm serious. I noticed the same thing," said Leader in a rare moment of sincerity while addressing Mantis. "Those women are basically wrapped up in a burlap sack sixteen hours a day, and the only way they have to show any individuality is their eyes. Beautiful - a lot of 'em."

"Yeah," added Jamie, also mesmerized by the cubes of frozen water shining in his glass. He reached out and grasped the side of the glass, feeling the refreshing cold of its contents. *I'll never take simple things for granted again,* he promised himself.

"Like last week when I was at your mother's house, Mantis...," began Leader, veering away from his momentary lapse into sincerity, "...now there's a lady with nice eyes."

"Why do I even bother?" moaned Mantis, giving a surreptitious middle finger salute to the grinning Leader. But he was smiling, too.

Warden was the first to notice the man working his way toward their table. Without looking directly at him, he could see that the man's eyes were focused on their table as he moved across the restaurant. *Both hands are visible. Good,* Warden noted as his shoulders and forearms involuntarily tensed. He unconsciously swung his knees slightly to the side of his chair, as he turned toward the approaching figure so as to be able to reach his feet quickly, if needed.

"Excuse me," offered the slightly balding, thirtyish man as he approached. Every face at the table turned toward him, all expressions gone flat as each team member quickly evaluated this interloper. *Slightly overweight civilian, hands in view, no bulges under clothing...*

"My family and I are sitting over there." The man gestured to a seven year old boy and an attractive woman with auburn hair sitting in a booth along the far wall of the restaurant. "Our waitress mentioned to us that you men are just back from the Middle East."

"Yessir, we are," replied Warden cautiously, unsure if this was some tree-hugger he was going to have to deal with. *Just keep your hands in front of you,* he mentally commanded, trying to present a passive front.

"Well, I really admire all of you for what you do. I was wondering if my son could come over and meet you. He's really interested in soldiers and all that, which is why we stopped here on our way to Orlando. He really wants to see a genuine soldier," the man beamed hopefully.

"That leaves you out, dough boy," Leader sniped in a side comment to Mantis, to which he received only a mild shake of the young sergeant's head in response.

"Sure, Sir," replied Warden pleasantly, still closely monitoring the man's every movement. "We'd be happy to say howdy, if he'd like to come on over."

"Great, that's awfully nice of you." The man turned and waved to his son over to the soldiers' table. Warden unconsciously evaluated the man's back as he turned. *No bulge at the beltline under his shirt – no pistol; no lump at the bottom of his slacks: he's clean.*

The little boy sprinted across the restaurant toward the team, a big smile on his face. Behind him, his mother's movement as she reached into the big straw bag next to her caught Leader's attention, *No surprises, lady,* he thought, tensing against his better judgment. His gaze remained fixed on her until she produced a small pocketbook, which she began to fumble through. *Relax, Pete,* he chided himself. *America, remember?* Despite the self-admonishment, he again fixed his eyes upon her as she returned the pocketbook to the large bag until her hand came out empty.

"This is Jonathan," declared the father proudly, as his son panted up to his side and hugged his leg. "Johnny, these men are real soldiers; they've just returned from the war in Iran." The boy stood clinging to his father, silent, with large eyes gazing at the men as if Superman had been sitting in their place.

"…umm, Iraq, actually," corrected Warden as he threw a quizzical look at Leader.

"Oh, sorry," laughed the father. "I always get that mixed up. Those countries over there are all pretty much the same to me." Leader resisted the urge to roll his eyes, feigning sudden interest in his water glass.

"Howdy, son," volunteered Warden, relaxing enough to smile and extend a rough, calloused hand toward the boy to shake. The boy gently shook the massive hand. "I'm Sergeant Warden. This is Sergeant Leader, Sergeant Mantis, Specialist Cooper, PFC Jamie, and Private Ridlin." Each of the soldiers stood and reached across the table to shake the dazzled boy's hand.

"Wer…Were you in combat?" the boy asked, his eyes round and bulging out of his freckled face from beneath reddish brown hair.

"Some of the time, son," Warden replied kindly, thinking of his daughter Amy waiting for him in Texas, as he looked at the boy's innocent face. They were roughly the same age.

"Did you kill anyone?" the boy blurted, his eyes bulging even further. The boy's father stood next to him, an oblivious smile on his face, waiting for the reply.

Directing his blurred vision back toward the sprinter, Warden sensed… something in his hand…detonator? Without further hesitation Warden brought his weapon to his shoulder and squeezed the trigger.

The Syrian leaned further out of the minaret to get a clean shot at the boy. Leader spotted the movement and traversed the SAW barrel upward and to the right, letting loose a burst of 5.56 mm rounds as he reached the window in his sight line. Caught fully across the chest with the burst, the insurgent tumbled backwards into the tower, disappearing from sight.

"Jamie, grease that damn Haji!," roared Warden from his position in the ditch as the man cut back toward the village. "This ain't no damn carnival game." Jamie calmed his breathing and this time led the running target, slowly squeezing the trigger, as he kept pace with the man's movement.

CRACK! Ridlin looked down the barrel as the top of the target's head blew into a red spray of hair-covered fragments as his round found its mark. The body pitched heavily into the dirt, giving an involuntary kick before lying quiet.

"Did you kill anyone, mister?" the boy repeated again in a high voice, as Warden and the others returned to the present.

"Uhm,... no, son. A lotta' soldiers never even fire their weapon in a war." *No way I'm goin' there with this kid,* thought Warden. *What the hell's wrong with his father, lettin' him ask a question like that? The war ain't an amusement park attraction.*

A momentary look of disappointment passed across the boy's face.

"Better luck next time, huh?" suggested the father with a nasal laugh, not noticing the cold wave that had washed across the table.

Hoping to break the dark mood that had suddenly descended on his team, Warden reached into his pants' pocket and pulled out his wallet. Thumbing quickly through it, he produced a one-thousand dinar Iraqi bill he had been carrying with him. Handing it to the boy, he lightly joked, "Now ya' have a thousand Iraqi dinars. You're rich."

The boy took the bill with the prominent face of Saddam Hussein on the front, looking at it in absolute wonder. "What's a thousand dinars in real money?" asked the father, likewise marveling at the exotic currency in his son's small hands.

"'Bout thirteen cents," offered Leader, returning from his own memory.

"Thanks, mister," gushed the boy, admiring his new treasure.

"Are you gonna' be a soldier when you grow up?" asked Jamie from across the table.

"I'd like to…," said the boy with the honesty of youth, still turning the precious bill over and over in his hands. "…but my mom says that's for people who can't do anything else, and she wants me to go to college to become something."

"Nice," Leader said flatly, looking at the now non-smiling, nervous father.

"Um, Jonathan, I think you must have mixed up what mommy meant," the father laughed nervously, trying desperately to not make eye contact with anyone at the table as he feigned continued interest in the Iraqi money.

"Uh-huh, daddy," insisted the boy with righteous certainty. "When Ashley's boyfriend joined the Marines, Mommy said it was a waste 'cause he was really smart and had 'tential."

All color left the man's already pale features. "I, umm, I'm really sorry," he stammered, looking at Warden pleadingly. "You know our whole family really admires what you men have done. Really!"

"Just so they don't have to do it, right?" snapped Leader, bitterly.

"Pete," cut in Warden, shooting him a look. "Sir, it was nice meeting y'all," he added in a forced pleasant tone. "Me and the boys need to get back to our celebration, if ya' don't mind. I hope you and your family have a real good time in Orlando."

"Thanks…thanks again. I really do admire what you men do," the father added lamely. "Everyone does. I think he just misunderstood, you know?" He nodded weakly at his son, who was still marveling over the gift in his hands — oblivious to the tension of the adults around him.

"No problem, sir. It's our job. Have a good day." Warden swung himself back toward the rest of his team, indicating that the conversation was over. He watched the man and his son return to their own table, and then observed the quiet but animated conversation between the husband and wife. The entire family left the restaurant a few minutes later.

"Nothing like thanks for a job well done," smirked Leader.

"Yeah," said Mantis. "But I'm bettin' that ain't gonna' be a real pleasant drive 'tween here and Disney World."

Chapter 3
The Homecoming

"Ladies and gentlemen, welcome to Dallas-Fort Worth International Airport. Please remain seated, with your seat belts fastened, until the aircraft is fully parked at the gate, and the Captain turns off the fasten seat belt sign," directed the flight attendant on American Airlines Flight 3422.

Warden looked out the window into the dusk, watching the refueling trucks and luggage carts scurrying across the tarmac as the aircraft bringing him from Charlotte taxied toward the terminal. He had remained at Fort Bragg a week later than the rest of his unit on the excuse of coordinating weapons turn-in and cleaning. The delay had allowed him the opportunity to see a civilian doctor off-post to explore his headaches and blurred vision without being kept on active duty indefinitely – a risk if he went to the post clinic.

The doctor had checked his eyes, run some tests, and told Warden what he already knew: "You've had your bell rung too many times and probably have a compound concussion. The eyesight will likely correct itself over the next few weeks. The headaches…well, that depends on what's going on inside that melon of yours. Your brain has been bounced around inside your skull, and we're only going to know with time. When there are multiple traumas over a short period like you experienced, it's hard to predict how the body will react. If you're still experiencing vision problems thirty days from now, you need to get a CT scan done."

I thought I'd be more excited, Warden mused as his plane turned sharply toward the terminal gate. He contemplated his return after a one-year combat tour in Iraq and fifteen months away from home. *Been livin' for this moment every day for over a year and now that it's here I feel…empty…numb. What the hell's wrong with me?* he chided himself.

He knew that somewhere in the broad windows of the terminal his wife and five-year old daughter, Amy, were waiting for him. *It'll be good,* he tried to convince himself. *I need to put on a happy face for 'em.*

"Look, we need to meet tonight. Hey, I don't care what time I get to the hotel. This is a big deal. We need to close this thing or there'll be hell to pay."

The overweight man with the bad comb-over sitting on Warden's left had roused from his sleep. Warden had been thankful when the man had quickly pounded a scotch shortly after takeoff and fallen into a noisy slumber. He had already received enough wide-eyed looks for traveling in his green Class-A uniform on this flight and was not in the mood for chit-chat. *People act like they've never seen a uniform,* he groused inwardly.

Behind him Warden could hear another too-loud phone conversation starting.

"Well, how late is she going to be? This has been a long day and I want to get home… Well, why did she take the Lexus? She knows it's been acting up…"

Warden looked about the plane as other cell phones sprang to life. *When did this happen?* he wondered. *These people are in such a damn hurry they can't wait to get off the plane before they call?*

"…Oh and then you know what she said? She said that if Ryan gets voted off she's going to have all of her friends call the station and complain! Isn't that a scream? Gawd, she's such a freak sometimes!"

The teenage girl sporting the Goth makeup in the row behind him had sprung into cellular action. *This is Texas, isn't it?* Warden asked himself.

As the plane eased to a halt at the gate several of the passengers jumped to their feet and began digging in the overhead storage bins. The pilot's baritone voice on the intercom stopped some of them: "Ladies and Gentlemen, this is Captain Howard. Thank you for flying with us today, and welcome to Dallas-Fort Worth International Airport. I would like to ask your patience for a couple more minutes to remain in your seats. The seat belt sign is still lit if you will notice."

Several passengers who were already digging for their carry-ons in the overhead compartments looked about with irritated expressions before reluctantly sitting back down. Several others ignored the request and continued to paw aggressively through the overhead bins.

The Captain continued: "We have the special privilege today of bringing an American hero home and would ask you to show him respect by permitting him to debark the aircraft before we do passenger unloading."

Warden looked down at his palms and rubbed his sweaty fingers together. *Why did I volunteer for this? I could have just quietly gone in civilian clothes my ownself.* Several people in the rows near him were staring now and whispering to each other. *Well… you know why, so just quit whining.*

"Jeezus Christ!" the balding man on Warden's left bleated into the phone. "They're delaying us again! Look, you need to have everyone in the conference room no later than 8:30, got it?"

The flight attendant with the kind smile who had greeted Warden when he first came aboard came down the aisle and knelt beside him. "Are you ready, Sergeant?" she asked in a soft voice.

"Yes ma'am," Warden replied, unbuckling his belt and slowly rising to his feet.

"Yeah, well we have some Army guy on the plane and the airline is throwing him a party," rasped the increasingly nasally voice of Warden's seat partner, as he tossed the NCO a dirty look. "Yeah, yeah, he's a war hero or somethin',…I know…I know! …They don't care," he pleaded to his unseen audience.

Warden retrieved his half-full canvas "A-Bag" from the overhead compartment before turning back to the stewardess. He resisted the impulse to look back at the annoying salesman. "I'm ready ma'am," he told her.

"Who knows?" said the teenager's voice from behind him. "Some Air Force guy is getting special treatment. Look, I'll be there as soon as I can."

Warden followed the flight attendant forward along the aisle that was now a thousand yards long. The other passengers looked at him quickly and then looked away so as to not stare. As he entered the first class compartment, one lone passenger began to clap; then another; and a third.

God, not now, thought Warden.

The other passengers slowly joined in and the cacophony of applause grew. Embarrassed for himself and the others, Warden reached out to touch the sleeve of the flight attendant. She turned back toward him. "They don't understand," Warden pleaded to her moist eyes.

"I know. It's OK," she said with a reassuring squeeze of her hand on his forearm.

The attendant turned and led the tall soldier out the now open front door of the aircraft onto the extended ramp. Rather than turning to the right to continue up the mobile walkway, she reached for a yellow door on the left, a dozen feet from the aircraft's exit. "Authorized Personnel Only" was emblazoned across the thick glass in large red letters. Opening the door, she stepped out onto a metal framed staircase and descended toward the tarmac. Warden followed, feeling his pulse throbbing in his temples.

At the bottom of the stairway, beneath the belly of the aircraft, six soldiers in the same Class-A uniform waited in two rows of three at the position of attention. The ranking soldier, an E-5 "Buck" Sergeant, stepped from the ranks and extended his hand to greet Warden. "Welcome home, Sergeant."

"Thanks, Sergeant," Warden replied, returning the firm grip. He glanced up at the windows of the aircraft and saw the rows of impatient faces pressed up against the glass. The man in the cell phone could now be seen gesturing toward the military gathering, as he vigorously spoke into his hand.

Warden turned back to the younger sergeant with one word: "Proceed."

The aircraft's cargo bay had already been opened by the waiting ground crew. Two men wearing yellow safety vests and headphones waited in the shadows just inside. Beside them, a long silver box had been gently removed from its securing straps and slid to the edge of the door. Without a word the young sergeant climbed onto the elevated cargo platform, stooped and entered the belly of the aircraft. He quickly unfolded the triangular cloth bundle that had been pressed tightly under his left arm to his side. He carefully draped the flag over the box and exited to rejoin his comrades as the airline employees gently guided the coffin out into the warm Texas evening breeze.

As the hydraulic lift lowered the young soldier's remains toward the tarmac, Warden felt someone on his left. A pale young woman wearing a dark dress was escorted by a young lieutenant. The honor guard began executing their role as pallbearers, carrying the remains of their brother to a dark hearse waiting several dozen yards away. As the flag-draped coffin slowly passed him, Warden snapped a salute and held it at the corner of his eyebrow. Unwillingly, his eyes drifted up to the round portholes of the aircraft.

Faces. Frozen. Not a word being spoken. The fat face of his seatmate filled the window behind the wing, his jaw hanging open while the phone dangled uselessly several inches from his ear.

A small sound reached up to him. "Di…did you know my husband, Sergeant?" the young woman asked, her voice cracking slightly.

"Not personally, ma'am," he replied, lowering his salute and turning to meet her gaze, instantly regretting the disappointment he saw to his response. "But I can tell you for certain that he was an American hero. And I'm proud to have served in the same Army with him."

Tears welled in her eyes as she smiled bravely, reaching out to take Warden's hand in her own. "Thank you for bringing him home," she whispered, before her voice choked into silence.

"It was my honor, ma'am," he replied, feeling his own throat tightening. *Her face looks like she's hardly old enough to be out of high school - 'ceptin' the eyes. They're for an older woman,* he thought.

She squeezed his hand and tried to force another smile, before turning back to the Lieutenant. "I'm ready," she breathed.

"Sergeant, thank you for your service and for volunteering for this mission," the Lieutenant said as he took the young widow's arm in his. "I understand this is your return home flight from Iraq. It's quite a sacrifice for you to volunteer for this duty as well."

"Sir, the only sacrifice here is what this young troop and his family did for this country," he replied, tilting his head slightly toward the hearse.

The Lieutenant nodded in understanding. *These days even the lieutenants get it,* Warden realized.

Warden saluted the young officer whose right arm was now gripped like a lifeline by the young widow, preventing him from returning the courtesy.

No other words were necessary or appropriate. The Lieutenant and his charge slowly retreated toward a limo waiting behind the hearse into which the flag-draped coffin had now been loaded. He walked with a slow, steady pace, trying not to rush the woman whose legs appeared ready to buckle at any second.

Warden stood, alone, and numbly stared across the flight line into the growing darkness. Green runway lights twinkled in the distance, and the warm breeze, scented by jet exhaust, blew lightly on his face. He breathed deeply through his nose, gathering strength for the next step of his journey. His mind was empty – a technique he had mastered over the past several months to deal with the overwhelming situations that were the daily fare of life in Iraq.

The flight attendant had quietly returned and was again by his side. "Your family is waiting, Sergeant. Let's get you home, huh?"

Warden didn't move. *I got a family to go home to. Abu is dead. This girl's husband is dead. The Haji at the truck stop is dead. I get to go home. It doesn't make any sense.*

"Sergeant?" The flight attendant inquired carefully.

Warden turned and looked at the concerned face next to him. "Ya' know, he wasn't a hero at all," Warden confessed in his low Texas drawl. "He was just another scared kid who happened to be standing in the chow line at Camp Bucca when some Haji dropped a mortar round on him. Complete fluke. Never knew what hit 'em."

"Look up at those windows, Sergeant."

Warden looked up and saw the same faces were still pressed against the glass: The Goth; the fat, impatient salesman. "Yes'm, I see 'em. They'll be gone the second they get released off that aircraft to their busy lives and forget all 'bout this."

"The pilot released them five minutes ago."

Warden stood dumb – he felt his cheeks burn.

"I didn't know," he murmured.

"I know. And I know most of those folks don't fully understand what you and that young man did over there. But it doesn't mean they don't respect it. Now, you've had a long trip and there's the most beautiful little girl up those stairs who's asking for her daddy. Do you think we can help her out?"

"Yes'm, I think we can. Thanks for squarin' me away."

"No problem. Move out, soldier," she added with a pat on Warden's broad back.

Chapter 4
The Gauntlet

Rick Smith didn't like this stretch of highway. There were seven different bridge overpasses along this remote stretch, and each one provided a potential ambush site. Each was a potential choke point where an otherwise quiet morning could be ripped into a storm of fire and jagged metal. The Hajis regularly used highway overpasses to target lightly protected convoys. In an otherwise flat and featureless region, they were about as perfect man-made terrain as you could wish for.

The *Hajis put a man with an RPG[5] on the reverse slope of the overpass,* Smith reminded himself. *The RPG man hits the lead vehicle as it exits from beneath the bridge, causing the convoy to jam up behind the stricken vehicle. IEDs then detonate, taking out any vehicles unwise enough to cluster up beneath the false protection of the bridge.* Smith's thoughts went back to the destroyed US convoy they had come upon north of Al Hillah several months ago, so shredded by a chain of IEDs that body parts were being gathered in trash bags.

Smith's thoughts turned – as they so often did these days – to the morning outside the village of Al Salaam when his own team had been ripped by a remotely-detonated artillery shell in the opening move of an insurgent ambush. The memory of Jamie and Ridlin sprinting through enemy fire to reach the wounded major was so clear that he felt he could reach out and touch it if he wanted to. Indeed, he felt he could step right back into the scene with all its dust, blood, sweat and noise.

Ridlin sprinting straight for the destroyed HMMWV oblivious to the enemy small arms fire all around him; Warden angrily gesturing for the MEDEVAC helicopter to land; the tight expression on Leader's face as he watched the village for enemy survivors of the Cobra gunship assault that had saved them; the nauseating smell of burnt flesh wafting out from the rubble...

Did I do enough that day? I should have been in the lead vehicle, Smith chastised himself. *I always let Bill take all the risks. A good deputy keeps the boss out of trouble. My fault...*

The approaching overpass shook him from his memories, and Smith refocused upon his immediate surroundings. *Sometimes a lone sniper would simply lie flat on top of the bridge,* Smith recalled, *targeting the rear vehicles of the convoy as they appeared beneath him.* The prone elevation of the sniper and direction of travel of the vehicles would render any return fire largely ineffective. *Nuthin' I can do about that,* he considered as he gazed eastward, along his path of travel.

It was going to be another hot one today. There had been no rain for three months, as the caked dust on the windscreen attested, and there was no relief in sight. The sun was not yet fully above the horizon this morning, but its glare was already limiting his vision as he approached the last of the threatening structures on this route. The dawn backlit the bridge, creating a silhouette that washed out any detail around it. The orange and purple glow increased and reached out toward him through the mouth of the underpass.

Damn it, Smith thought as his anxiety heightened with the increasing glare. Sweat ran in multiple rivulets down the sides of his torso: *I can't see anything.* He held his left hand in front of his face to shade his eyes, without much improvement. He could still see only the broadest, dark outline of the approaching overpass. *Sun is in the perfect spot to make sure I'm blind. I'm screwed.*

His T-shirt was already soaked with perspiration at this early hour from his cumulative reaction to the six overpasses already behind him. *I know it's just a piece of goddamn concrete,* he tried to convince himself. *Nuthin' is gonna' happen.* Sweat continued to stream down his sides as if mocking him.

Smith realized that he was within small arms range now, subconsciously gauging the distance to the bridge. *They'd never hit me this far out, though. Wouldn't want to give a warning; gimme' a chance to avoid the trap.* His breathing quickened as the sun's rays climbed over the horizon and reached out for him. He could feel his heart pound, and he reached down to wipe each of his moist palms against the tops of his BDU[6] trousers.

Three hundred yards to the overpass: Nothing.

Two hundred yards: Smith tightened his grip on the steering wheel.

One hundred yards: No movement.

In this final stretch, Smith accelerated his truck out of habit and training, so as to not provide a steady target for anyone zeroing in on him. With the roar of his engine echoing from the concrete walls of the underpass, he shot out the far side into the growing dawn. No gunfire reached out for him. No rocket screamed through the thin air to validate his anxiety. The desert was quiet.

He was soaked through.

Smith shook his head and glanced backward at the sunlit gate as it faded in his side mirror. *Not today,* he thought. Smith shivered as the sweat now cooling against his sides chilled him, and he relaxed his grip on the wheel slowly, stretching his fingers and palms. *Breathe,* he reminded himself, drawing the dry air into his aching lungs.

Ahead he could see the lights of a town slowly fading in the otherwise dim flatlands about him. He took another deep breath and let it out slowly. The highway sign informed him that he was nearing his destination – "Route 335 - Amarillo 6 Miles."

I hope someone's fired up the coffee pot before I get to the Reserve Center, Smith thought. *I could use a pick-me-up.*

Chapter 5
The Party

As the brigade's new S1⁷ officer, Captain Smith was responsible for promotions, personnel records, and awards. He and his small staff had spent the past two weeks preparing today's official Welcome Home ceremony for the 538th. The event had followed the predictable pattern of such events: canned patriotic speeches about duty and sacrifice from local politicians who had never found military service personally convenient and a farewell address from Colonel Hermann, who was relinquishing command following the unit's redeployment.

The ceremony was largely a check-the-box event for the brigade, marking the "proper and official" return of the unit. Its soldiers – drawn from units from Texas to Connecticut – had quickly dispersed to their homes after being released from Fort Bragg. Smith was relieved that the event had largely gone off smoothly and was now winding down. Even Ridlin's gaffe in tripping and dropping the colors had not derailed the event. Several local television affiliate crews still milled about the drill hall, asking the troops such insightful questions as "Bet it was hot over there, huh?" Smith detached himself from this throng for a few minutes to clear his head.

Smith spotted Command Sergeant Major Woods standing with his arms crossed against the far wall of the drill hall, surveying the festivities through narrowed eyes. Smith had come to admire Woods' professionalism during their deployment: Woods had served as Hermann's Command Sergeant Major in Iraq, which meant that he was the "Old Man's" primary advisor on all issues relating to the unit's NCOs and enlisted personnel. It had been an unenviable position. Unlike in a combat line unit, many of the senior, part-time officers in Civil Affairs had little knowledge of how to utilize the leadership capabilities of a strong NCO. Woods had demonstrated a talent for educating these officers in a quiet and nonthreatening manner that did not bruise their egos. His most valuable contribution during the 538th's deployment had been in insulating his enlisted troops from the internecine warfare between the sixteen colonels and twenty three lieutenant colonels who staffed the top-heavy headquarters.

In civilian life Woods was a detective on the Texas State Attorney General's drug task force. In his military career he was one of the few remaining senior NCOs who had served in Viet Nam. He had begun his career as a draftee, conducting long-distance recon missions in enemy territory. Few knew – though Smith was among these due to his access to the personnel files – that Woods had two Purple Hearts and a Bronze Star for Valor amongst his long list of awards. Woods himself never spoke of these decorations. This assignment with the 538th was to be his last before he reached his mandatory retirement date; the magic day upon which the Army decreed that an individual was simply too old to die for their country.

"Mornin', Sergeant Major," offered Smith as he walked up to the senior NCO.

"Mornin', Sir."

"Not gonna' join the party?"

"I'm fine right here. Thanks, Sir," replied Woods evenly.

Smith joined the sergeant major in supporting the cinder block wall with his back, watching the swarm of local press and politicians amongst the troops and their families, shaking hands, back-slapping, and congratulating the soldiers on a job well done.

"Nice to be appreciated, huh, Sergeant Major?" asked Smith. "This'll make the men feel good, don't ya' think?"

"Hmmph," grunted Woods, continuing his observation without expression.

Smith had spent enough time around Woods to know that his "Hmmph" conveyed dissatisfaction with the current state of affairs.

Smith glanced sideways at Woods and saw the lines framing the stoic NCO's grey eyes deepen. Woods' salt and pepper hair was cut to perfect military standard, as usual. "And '*hmmph*' means exactly what today, Sergeant Major?"

Woods didn't turn his head. Without changing expression, he said, "Sir, I'm not lookin' to piss in anyone's punch bowl, but since you asked, I gotta' tell you this is all bullshit."

Smith had known the Sergeant Major to be a man who kept an even keel and a decent sense of humor even in the worst of times. Woods' condemnation of a simple welcome home ceremony was a surprise.

"Why's that?" Smith asked.

Woods looked about the room. "Take a look at Jamie with that female reporter, sir," he indicated with a nod of his head. Smith spotted Private First Class Jamie being questioned by a pretty young reporter from the local FOX affiliate. She wore the empty smile that seemed to characterize the breed, and her bright red suit provided the camera a nice contrast with her perfectly styled, shoulder-length blonde hair. Woods continued, "He's all smiles and sound bites for her 30-second report tonight. He thinks these people really give a damn about what he did over there."

"And they don't?

"He's entertainment, Sir, pure and simple. People want to see a young soldier in uniform say something patriotic so they can feel good about themselves as they switch the channel to *The Price is Right*. That's the whole war to them."

"Well, there's nothing wrong with makin' people feel good about these troops comin' home, is there?" asked Smith.

"Sir, I'm just an old warhorse and you should just ignore me. But what I see in all this is people celebratin' the fact that someone else went to clean out the drains and they don't hafta' be bothered with it."

"That's pretty cynical there, Sergeant Major. Need a nap?" Smith joked.

"Maybe so, sir," Woods replied, showing the first hint of a smile. "I just know that guys like Jamie probably have a year or eighteen months before Uncle Sugar's gonna' ship his ass back to Iraq, and these same hangers-on will show up again then to give a heartfelt farewell and be secretly thinkin', 'Thank God it's not me or mine.'"

"Well, that's a natural enough reaction, I suppose…"

"Sir, don't get me wrong. I'm not naive. Been humpin' a ruck for over thirty years and it's no great revelation that there always has been and always will be just a small number of guys willin' to spill their guts in some Haji hell hole, 'stead of just singing 'America' at a Memorial Day picnic once a year."

"Well if anyone gave me those choices I'd choose singing 'America,' too," Smith joked.

Woods chuckled appreciatively. "Yeah, I suppose – and yet here you are anyway – on your weekend. You're not sleepin' in this morning and then goin' out to play golf."

"I suppose…I don't know. It's just natural to me. I can't blame those who don't find this worthwhile for themselves. Besides, golf is for wimps."

"Ha! Yep, not everyone's cut out for this racket, Sir, and that's the way it's always been. It's just the dishonesty that bothers me, I suppose. This is all just for someone else's entertainment," Woods waved his hand toward the buzzing crowd. "The men deserve better than to be a sound bite."

"I don't know, Sergeant Major. All I've seen is support from the public everywhere I look. People are givin' up their seats on planes for young soldiers, buyin' them a drink, shakin' their hand, and thankin' 'em for their service. There's a lot of real support out there."

"Sir," said Woods coolly, as he turned to look into Smith's face for the first time, "*Real* support would be gettin' their asses down to the recruiting station."

Smith chuckled at the senior NCO's unwillingness to budge an inch. "It's a volunteer army, Sergeant Major. The country's accepted a small professional force doin' the empire's dirty work these days."

"Granted, Sir, but even in the past at least the nation's leaders put in their time. Now you have guys with no real military background sendin' these kids off like it was a big damn game of *Risk*. Christ, Sir, how many of these politicians out there…" – he gestured toward one state representative having his picture taken with Jamie – "…are sending their kids off to fight in this so-called 'fight against terror?' If it's as damn important as the NCA[8] keeps sayin,' why aren't their kids wearin' a uniform? It's the hypocrisy that chaps me. The country's survival's at stake, they claim, but 'oh, excuse me, I've got another call on line two,'" he mimicked. "It makes ya' wonder if some of it isn't just window dressing."

"Tell me how you really feel, Sergeant Major," Smith joked, again trying to lighten the mood.

Woods' reply was interrupted by the swift approach of the lady in red, who had spotted a stationary target of opportunity. Her cameraman scurried behind her to catch up.

"Excuse me, Sergeant?" inquired the reporter. "PFC Jamie said you would be a good person to give a statement on behalf of the command about your recent mission."

"Did he now?" asked Woods evenly, silently promising himself to drop Jamie for fifty push-ups as soon as this circus was over. He looked over the blonde's head, scanning the crowd for the young troop who had just set him up and then slipped away.

"Let me step out of your fifteen minutes of fame, Sergeant Major," added Smith, shifting a couple of steps sideways with a grin of anticipation.

"Ooh, you're a *Major?*" gushed the young reporter, quickly scratching some notes into a notepad she held in her delicately manicured hand.

"*Sergeant Major*, ma'am," replied Woods flatly. The temptation to excuse himself from this young woman's presence was tempered by the direction of the new brigade commander – Colonel Burr – that everyone was to be "fully cooperative with the press today."

Just another reason to dislike that man, Woods thought.

"Ok," she replied slowly, scratching a correction into her pad. "And your name is Woods, correct? W-O-O-D-S?"

"Yes, ma'am," replied Woods stiffly, catching Smith smiling at his discomfort out of the corner of his eye.

"And what is your job in the unit?" she asked, thrusting her microphone below Woods' chin. The glare of the TV camera's strobe caused the old NCO to squint.

"My job is to ensure these troops are ready to kill our enemies, ma'am."

The young reporter's eyes widened slightly as she stammered at the unexpected response, "B...but you're a civilian affairs unit, right? That means you don't really fight, right? ...You like, build schools and things like that?"

"*Civil* Affairs, ma'am. The primary job of *any* US soldier is to defend this nation by killing those enemies that the President identifies as a threat to this nation. My job is to make sure these troops kill them efficiently and in great numbers; once that's done, if we can construct a school or two, that's just fine."

"So...so all of these young men and women here today are in uniform to kill people, Sergeant? Is that what you are saying?" she challenged, attempting to recover her professional demeanor.

"*Sergeant Major*, ma'am. Yes, ma'am; this is not the Peace Corps. The Army's job is to destroy our nation's enemies. If we can do that by digging a well to win some hearts and minds, that's fine. If we can do that by blowing the heads off hostile personnel, that's even better."

"The young people I've talked to today don't look like killers, ma... major sergeant," the reporter stuttered. "They're perfectly *normal,*" she countered, an edge to her voice.

"They *are* normal, ma'am. That's discipline and training you see. This is not a gang of violent thugs. This is a highly trained group of military professionals, trained to kill and to exercise restraint, where appropriate. Most of them have college at one level or 'nother. They're no different than you – right up until someone sets off a bomb or pulls a weapon. When that happens you'll run away from the danger; they'll run *toward* it."

The young reporter's mouth sought to form another question, but found none. "Umm, thank you," she replied half-heartedly, signaling to her cameraman to stop filming.

"My pleasure, ma'am," Woods replied, his face still emotionless.

Turning, the reporter spoke quietly to her cameraman as they moved away, "Well, that wasn't very *happy.* I don't think we can use any of that. It'll upset the viewers."

Smith sidled back up to the Sergeant Major to watch the pair retreat. Woods resumed his relaxed lean against the wall with his arms crossed across his chest. There was a slight twinkle in his eye.

"You enjoyed that way too much, Sergeant Major," Smith said quietly, smiling.

Woods tilted his head slightly toward the officer with a thin smile and one raised eyebrow. "Just followin' orders, Sir."

Chapter 6
The Scheme

"Doug! Congratulations on your command," twanged the high pitched voice of Colonel Walter Rabbit through the telephone.

"Thanks, Walt," replied Colonel Douglas Burr, the newly appointed commander of the 538th Civil Affairs Brigade. He leaned back in his creaky swivel chair with his feet elevated on the metal government desk before him. "It's going to be nice to control my own fate for a change."

Along with Rabbit, Burr had been among the group of senior officers who Brigadier General Joseph Merdier had swept from his higher headquarters at the 42nd Civil Affairs Command at the start of the war. Merdier had used his subordinate unit's deployment as the opportunity for a military "garage sale," to clean his own headquarters of a dozen colonels who had become too inconvenient or ambitious for him to keep around. Burr had been at the top of the list of those whose appetites were too large for Merdier's table.

Rather than commanding an intelligently organized military unit, therefore, the 538th's previous commander, Colonel Hermann, had been turned into a daycare provider, spending his deployment trying to placate the competing egos of Merdier's fractious minions – many of whom were senior to him. Burr had served in the position of Deputy Commander of the 538th during the deployment, while using his position as a platform to second-guess Hermann's every move in backchannel criticism to Merdier. The result had been a fractious and demoralized unit where no command decision was the only safe decision to make.

The frustration of the leaderless troops who had deployed with the false hope of making a difference in the war had led one wag to create a fictitious "Order of the Blue Falcon" award that was periodically and secretly assigned to commemorate the worst self-promoting conduct of the unit's senior officers. Burr had held the record for longest consecutive possession of the fictitious distinction due to his proclivity to affix unearned combat patches[9] and awards on his uniform. Ironically, the happiest time for the 538th troops during the entire deployment had been at Christmas when Burr and the rest of the 42nd's colonels had contrived their own leave back to the States, leaving their enlisted troops alone in the desert. The temporary absence of the senior officers had made the holidays almost palatable.

Rabbit had served as the officer responsible for monitoring Iraqi government reform for the 538th during the deployment. After a couple initial missions into "Injun Country," including one infamous moment when he led his team through a minefield, Rabbit realized that his highest and best use was generating briefing slides from the relative safety of the base camp for the commanding general's staff in Baghdad. The fact that these slides bore little resemblance to the chaotic state of Iraq's provincial governments seemed not to trouble his superiors. They looked damn impressive, and provided a favorable foundation for hopeful reports from the field of substantial progress back to Washington. Rabbit's tenure as a PowerPoint Ranger had been sufficiently distinguished that he was now the Chief of Operations for the Civil Affairs Branch at Fort Bragg, North Carolina.[10]

Burr's opportunity for brigade command would likely not have arrived for some time, except for the fortuitous realignment of the Army Reserves after the first disorganized year of the Iraq War. In the bureaucratic reshuffling, the headquarters of the 538th CA Brigade had been relocated from Baltimore to Amarillo, Texas. The move had created an opening for Burr when the incumbent, Colonel Hermann, had declined to accept a 2,000-mile commute.

"So are you going to clean out all of the dead wood like you said?" Rabbit inquired, referencing the various personnel that Burr had taken a dislike to while serving as the unit's Number Two officer.

"I hope so. I do hope so – but I have to move cautiously, Walt. With the current state of the Reserves, I have to keep in mind that retaining personnel is the number one factor that Merdier is going to rate me on in my performance evaluation. If it's upright and taking nourishment, I need to keep it until I find another warm body to replace it. I don't want that old butcher sticking it to me because of bad manning reports."

Master Sergeant Gordon Winkle, Burr's "Secretary of the General Staff, or "SGS," opened the office door and entered with a sheaf of papers in hand for the commander's signature. As the 538th was only a colonel-level command, this was not an actual job slot in the organization, but this had not deterred Burr from creating such a position to serve him. Winkle had been found stored in a back office of the motor pool during a routine inventory, dusted off, and reassigned as Burr's secretary and doorkeeper. No one was sure when Winkle had first come to the unit or what his job was prior to Burr's assumption of command. His stooped posture, frail frame, and thin grey hair placed his age somewhere between 55 and 95 years old. The rumor in the lower enlisted ranks was that the Reserve Center had been built around Winkle one day while he was sleeping, and he had just elected to stay.

Winkle shuffled to Burr's side and laid the documents expectantly before the officer, raising a pen and his eyebrows in an inquiring look. "Get out," Burr ordered as he covered the mouthpiece with his right hand.

"Very good, Sir, I'll get right on that," Winkle replied evenly, withdrawing to his outer office while leaving the papers for possible future attention.

Rabbit continued his congratulations of Burr. "Well, good for you, Doug, is all I can say. If I were you I'd definitely work hard to keep those retention numbers up, though," he advised.

"What do you know, Walt?" From the smug tone in Rabbit's voice Burr could tell that he had some tidbit of information he had not yet shared.

"Well, you recall how we were extended in Iraq twice due to lack of replacements?"

"I seem to vaguely recall that, yesss…" replied the irritated Burr, waiting for Rabbit to get to the point.

"Well, things are not much better, and the 538th is already on the burner for the next rotation back into the box, probably early next year due to the ongoing troop shortage."[11]

Burr silently pondered the significance of this revelation. He had needed the bells and bangles that came with the unit's first combat deployment in his personnel file for future career advancement; but a second deployment was not part of his carefully crafted career plans. He had calculated that his receipt of a dubiously-granted Air Medal, as well as the Combat Action Badge that he and the other 42nd CACOM colonels had nominated themselves for – the justification being that they were in Kuwait during an enemy missile attack on a position thirty kilometers away – had sealed his likely future advancement to General. Another deployment would not significantly improve his chances and might even cause him to miss an opportunity on this side of the ocean.

"You still there, Doug?" inquired Rabbit.

"Yes, yes…," Burr replied briskly.

"There's more."

"Go ahead."

"Well, this is not to be repeated, but Major General Oldhaus is going to announce his retirement in October and Merdier has the inside track to take over as CAPOC commander."

"Really?" asked Burr slowly, with a slight lilt in his voice. The implications were obvious: if Merdier moved up, there would be a one-star opening at the 42nd CACOM as soon as he did. That was practically *now*. This could be an opportunity for Burr to vault into the general officer ranks within the next year at a fairly young age *and* avoid an undesirable repeat tour in Iraq. "That is *good* news," he acknowledged.

"Yeah, the water cooler talk up here is that if Merdier moves up then Colonel Martin at the 841st has the inside track to get his star," said Rabbit.

"Martin?" Burr spat angrily. "What has *Martin* accomplished? He sat his brigade on a nice safe post in West Baghdad for a year eating ice cream and getting fat. *I* have an Air Medal! Why does he have the inside track?"

"Well, it isn't a matter of his personal awards. It's what his *unit* accomplished. They were the most heavily engaged CA unit over there – came back with a half dozen Bronze Stars for valor and a couple of Purple Hearts from firefights. That caught some attention."

"What about us?" Burr whined. "Trevanathan managed to get his team chewed up pretty good in that ambush right before we left. We even had a KIA[12] – even though it was just a translator. Trevanathan and a couple of his NCOs got Bronze Stars."

"Six versus three; do the math," replied Rabbit lightly, amused at the unexpected agitation he had generated in his old comrade.

Burr's eyes became slits as he calculated his dilemma. *This may be the only general officer slot that opens up in the next five or six years. I can't let Martin steal it from me simply because he was lucky enough for a couple of his teams to get shot up.* Burr nervously licked at the corners of his mouth as his mind searched for an angle.

"Too bad, Doug," Rabbit tormented. "Not much of a chance for you to trump Martin's tally while sitting in Amarillo," he teased. "Guess you better start packing your A-Bag for the next rotation."

Burr's viper-like eyes darted anxiously across his desk top, coming to fix upon a folder Winkle had left behind labeled "Serious Incident Report." He absently flipped it open and ran his eyes over its contents. The report had not been generated until the unit had returned to the United States due to the proximity of the incident to the unit's redeployment. Burr tilted his head slightly as he focused upon the opening paragraph:

"On 08 APR 04 at 1018Z Team Jaguar, escorting Colonel Hermann to relinquish command in Baghdad, came under attack by a lone Iraqi terrorist. The terrorist was killed by small-arms fire by SFC Gus Warden, who promptly responding to the threat was…"

A smile crossed Burr's narrow features as he lifted the precious document.

"Doug, are you still there?" twanged Rabbit's voice.

"Oh, I'm here," replied Burr happily. "Tell me, Walt: what would it take to outshine three more Bronze Stars in the eyes of the powers-that-be?"

"It'd take a hell of a lot, I can tell you that much," replied Rabbit. "Probably a Silver Star …and as you know, no one in Civil Affairs has ever received one of those."

"Until now," replied Burr dryly. "Until now…"

Chapter 7
The Labyrinth

Smith's stomach knotted as he rapped on the Brigade Commander's door. "Come in!" ordered the deep Southern accent from the other side.

"Afternoon, Sir," greeted Smith without enthusiasm as he entered Burr's office. "The event is wrapping up downstairs." Smith knew Burr well from their recent deployment to Iraq and disliked him intensely. His hope to escape contact with Burr after returning to the States was crushed when Burr was named to follow Colonel Hermann in the brigade commander's chair.

Burr looked up from his *Ranger Joe's* catalog as Smith entered. He stared at his administrative officer as Smith closed the door and turned back toward him.

Smith hesitated at Burr's glare. Uncomfortable with the silence he asked, "You wanted to see me, Sir?"

"I'm waiting for you to report, Captain," Burr demanded, biting off his words.

Smith was stunned. *Jesus, this is just an informal meeting. This guy is really full of himself.* Quickly coming to attention, Smith snapped a salute and declared, "Captain Smith, reporting as ordered, Sir."

Burr eyed Smith closely, looking for any uniform infractions that he could exploit to put his S1 at an even greater disadvantage. Disappointed in finding none, he rendered a sloppy return salute and directed, "Be at ease."

Smith complied, placing his feet shoulder width apart with his hands clasped behind his back.

"Captain, you had a good reputation in Iraq, *even though* you kept some questionable company," Burr began, making a not-so-veiled reference to Smith's friendship with Major Trevanathan, the former brigade Judge Advocate, with whom Burr had frequently locked horns. "I want you to know that I don't intend to hold any of that against you," he explained, tapping the tips of his index fingers together before his pursed lips, as he scrutinized Smith.

He's got a lot of damn gall, thought Smith. The government reconstruction team that Smith and Trevanathan had been part of had driven more convoy miles than any other section of the brigade as they rode the circuit trying to breathe life into Iraq's corrupt and dysfunctional judicial system. Burr, who had been nicknamed "The POD" – short for "Prince of Darkness" – had spent his deployment behind a desk at Camp Babylon. *Burr could have mailed his deployment in,* Smith recalled.

"I'm going to show there's no hard feelings by giving you an opportunity to excel – that is, if you're the right man," sneered Burr.

"Sir?"

"I've often felt, Captain," Burr began with slow, measured speech, "That we did not do *justice* to the accomplishments of our men before leaving Iraq. In the recognition department, if you understand my meaning."

"Umm, not entirely, Sir."

"Let me clarify it for you then, Captain. The 841st CA brigade returned to Fort Bragg two weeks after we did. They had six troops who received Bronze Stars for valor and two others who received Purple Hearts. This is the sort of competition we're up against."

"*Competition*, Sir?"

"Don't be naive, Captain. *Competition* – just what I said. If Trevanathan had not managed to get your team shot up at the end of your last mission we would have come home with almost nothing. As it is, we collected only three Bronze Stars out of that, plus one lousy Purple Heart."

Smith felt the blood rushing to his face. "Sir, Major Trevanathan did not…"

"*Goddamnit,* don't interrupt me, Captain!" Burr barked, cutting him off. "That sort of disrespect may have worked in Trevanathan's little circus, but it damn well will not be tolerated here."

Smith gritted his teeth together, as he glared silently at Burr. He recalled the several times Trevanathan had led his team out of bad situations without a scratch. *Apparently getting your men shot up is the mark of success for glory seekers like Burr,* he realized with disgust.

Burr recovered his composure, remembering that he needed Smith's assistance if his scheme was to work. Softening his tone, he continued "Captain, you are a smart officer with a bright future. Everyone knows that. You and I need to work together as a team to make this the best brigade in USACAPOC."

What's his game? Smith pondered, remaining quiet. *He hates my guts. He needs something.*

"I was reviewing this Serious Incident Report involving Sergeant Warden. It was filed by you, wasn't it?" The POD shoved the folder across the desk toward Smith, where the signature page clearly showed Smith's signature.

"Yessir," replied Smith, glancing impassively at the document. *This isn't good,* he thought, feeling his palms moisten behind his back.

"This was quite a mission, wasn't it?" The POD inquired in an oily voice. "An assassination attempt upon a high ranking officer, foiled by Sergeant Warden's situational awareness and courage? We can't let this slip past without appropriate recognition, can we?" Burr noticed Smith shifting his weight uneasily.

"It…uh…was so near the end of the tour, Sir, that…uh…we basically decided not to make a big deal of it. Sergeant Warden isn't one much for personal glory." Smith felt like he had a glass head and Burr's beady eyes could see right into his brain. *What does he know?*

"I admire that type of humility as much as the next man, Captain. I really do. But it isn't fair to Sergeant Warden or the rest of the unit for his bravery to not be appropriately recognized. It isn't good for morale or *esprit*, is it?"

"I don't think he'll really…"

"You've made it quite clear what he thinks, Captain. But I am speaking of the good of the unit here. The good of the unit must always be paramount to individuals' desires – don't you agree?"

"Sometimes it isn't clear what is best for the good of the unit, Sir," Smith offered.

"Maybe to you, Captain, but it is abundantly clear to me. We have an NCO whose courage under enemy fire has not been appropriately recognized."

"The man had a knife, Sir."

"A *knife*? He attacked a convoy with a *knife*?" Burr's voice rose.

Smith shifted uneasily. He could feel the perspiration start to run down his body. "We....uh... believe that he was trying to, umm... use stealth to get near the Brigade Commander, Sir," Smith offered weakly.

Burr was not the world's best soldier, and his sense of duty was limited to what he might accomplish that would bring greater benefit to himself. His strongest gift – and what had enabled him to rise above his peers – was the ability to sense fear or weakness in others; Smith reeked of it. To The POD, every pore of the S1's body emitted the stink of fear. Burr did not know why, but he knew how to use it.

"Captain, I am convinced that you must be correct, as the only other alternative is one too disturbing to contemplate." He paused to let Smith's nervousness grow. "And so, what you are going to do for me is to go back to your desk and draft the necessary recommendation and narrative for Sergeant First Class Warden to be awarded the Silver Star for saving the life of Colonel Hermann. You will do so in a convincing manner that leaves no opportunity for the award to be denied or downgraded, am I clear?"

Smith knew he was trapped. To argue further would increase the likelihood that The POD would look deeper into the already weak story, placing everyone on that mission at risk of court-martial. The fact that an innocent Iraqi was shot was simply one of the unfortunate consequences of a messy war, where the line between combatants and civilians was often unclear. The truck driver's death alone would not have resulted in any adverse action, Smith knew. In a war where every civilian was a potential insurgent, the quick use of deadly force was generally recognized as necessary to stay alive. Revealing the mistake would have likely generated a formal inquiry, delaying their scheduled return home, but would not have led to a finding of criminal wrongdoing. But, the team's covering up the true nature of the shooting after the fact now placed them all on the chopping block for creating a false official report.

Smith also knew that the Silver Star was only a heartbeat away from the Congressional Medal of Honor, and was reserved for those extremely rare situations where a soldier engages in acts of valor so extraordinary and selfless that the loss of his own life was likely. The accidental shooting on the outskirts of Baghdad certainly did not qualify. Yet, there was only one possible response, and The POD had skillfully maneuvered him into it.

"Yes, Sir, I'll get right on it," replied Smith tautly. He brought himself to the position of attention and snapped a salute as a prelude to escaping Burr's lair.

"And Captain…," Burr's voice froze Smith, as he began to turn toward the door. "This is between you and me for now. I won't suffer any humble resistance from Warden or any of the others from that team that Trevanathan infused with his 'boy scout' view of the world. Understood?"

"Understood, Sir," replied Smith flatly, knowing he had been completely outmaneuvered.

Chapter 8
The Gate

Warden ran out onto the veranda of the Civilian Support Center seconds after the blast sent him diving out of his chair. Fifty yards away, the gate to the compound was a twisted heap of smoldering metal. A thick black cloud rose from just outside the walls. A helmetless Marine private, with fear in his eyes, ran up the three steps toward the NCO.

Warden grabbed him by the arm as he tried to pass. "Private, what happened?"

"Jesus Christ…oh, Jesus Christ," the private babbled, not looking at Warden while struggling to pull away. His unfocused eyes darted wildly in several directions. "Private, give me the sitrep," Warden insisted, raising his voice slightly as he squeezed the young troop's arm to get his attention.

"The Haji woman…that Goddamn Haji woman who brings the bread each day…" he heaved, gasping for breath.

"What about her?" Warden insisted.

"Blew herself all to hell. Oh, God!" The private doubled over and wretched heavily, his breakfast spilling onto the dusty porch.

Warden knew this was no time for hand-holding. He needed information fast to assess the scope of the threat. "Goddamn it, Private! Square yourself away and tell me what happened!"

The harshness of his voice triggered a trained response from the young Marine, who straightened himself and met Warden's eyes for the first time.

"She came up to the gate, just like always, Gunny. Nuthin' special. Had the bag of Haji bread over her shoulder – just like always. Then, *wham!*"

"Are you on gate guard?"

"No,…no,…I was at the water buffalo refillin' my canteen. I looked up and saw her talking to one of the Iraqi cops outside the gate. Then she just disintegrated in an orange flash. She…her…" The private looked away, bent over quickly and emptied the remaining contents of his stomach onto the dirt colored bricks.

"Shiit…," the young Marine groaned to himself as he slowly straightened again.

Warden waited impatiently for the young man to compose himself. Outside the destroyed gate he could see a crowd of Iraqis beginning to gather, milling about. A Marine quick reaction team bolted from a neighboring building toward them – weapons ready – their gear bouncing as they double-timed to meet any potential follow-on attack.

"She...uh, that is her body... the upper part... it just blew right over the wall and landed three feet away from me. Torn in half; no Goddamn arms or legs or nuthin', just..." The troop paused, swallowing hard to keep from retching again.

Warden surveyed the scene. The quick reaction force was directing the Iraqi civilians to move away from the gate. "Ok, Private, go report to the CO and let him know what's going on. Make sure an incident report gets transmitted to battalion ASAP. I'll go retrieve your helmet." Warden could see the helmet lying in the sand by the olive drab water trailer known as the "water buffalo." A few feet to one side he could see a smoldering pile of rags that had to be what was left of the Haji woman.

Warden had seen the woman several times during the past two weeks of his temporary detail to the Civilian Support Center in Nasiriyah. She usually showed up around lunchtime, bringing the warm pita bread that was a welcome diversion from the MREs and T-rations[13] that were the daily fare at this small outpost. Before the Americans had moved in, the small, walled compound had been a municipal building. It had been selected as a civil-military operations center due to its location on a major artery leading into the city center, its high walls, and its distance from surrounding buildings. The layout allowed the civil support team to be accessible while still providing them the ability to scrutinize anything approaching before it got too close. *Except the Haji woman…* Warden thought as he walked over to retrieve the Marine's helmet. *Good move on Haji's part – letting us get used to her and even welcome her food, and then using that trust against us. Gotta' give these bastards credit – they aren't dumb.*

The inevitable smell of charred flesh assaulted his nose as the wind shifted. He had first encountered the unique smell in Somalia during his "peacekeeping" tour with the 10[14] Mountain Division. Some days the smell hung over the Mog[14] like a blanket when the competing militias were tearing each other up. Warden quickly switched to mouth breathing, but the sour-sweet stench could almost be tasted, causing him to gulp deeply. *Great – I can't blow chow like that rookie back there, or I'll look like a fool.*

Warden quickened his pace, skirted the smoldering pile and snatched the helmet off the ground. The high-pitched whine of an ambulance siren grew as it approached from the city center. *No need for 'em to hurry. Nobody survived that blast.* He turned back toward the operations center. A sideways glance at the corpse showed him that the woman had landed face up – her dead eyes open to the sky. There was no blood visible, yet – the heat of the explosion had cauterized much as it tore her apart. He found he could not look away; the sight of her face peering up out of the small pile of smoking rags was hypnotic. Without meaning to, he was drawn to her corpse – to the scorched dead face. He could feel his stomach rising, but he fought it back.

He stopped when he was standing over her. Her lifeless eyes stared into his. Her eyebrows and lashes had burned away. He felt anger rising in himself. She was smiling. The corners of her mouth were twisted back in a twisted grin revealing a half dozen brown teeth behind blackened lips. *Smiling.*

"You bitch," Warden whispered, unable to look away. The woman continued to mock him as the first swarms of flies began to descend on her remains. *You damn people drive your country into the ground and then try to kill those who come to help ya'.* Warden gathered the little moisture in his mouth and spat fully onto her twisted features. "You terrorist bitch," he repeated, louder this time, as rage filled him.

"Let's go," she responded unexpectedly, clutching at his leg.

Warden jumped instinctively, grabbing at the hand holding him with his left, while his right hand fixed itself onto her throat. A guttural animal cry escaped his lips, as he bolted upright.

The wide-eyed fear on his wife's face caused him to hesitate, but the tight grip around her throat remained. Warden's heart slammed painfully against his ribcage, as he struggled to reconcile reality from memory.

"Are...are you alright?" Lil choked, her momentary lack of breath coming more from shock than his grip.

He looked about his bedroom. Their ranch; pictures of his daughter on the wall; the early morning sun streaming in the window. No threat. No dead Haji woman. Home. Warden jerked his hands away, shocked by his own lack of control. They were shaking. "Damn...," he declared, pulling his hands against his pounding chest. His soaked shirt clung to him.

"Are you OK?" Lil asked again, watching him carefully. "You're home…" she added quietly.

"Hon…I think I need to ask ya' not to grab me while I'm sleeping, OK?" he stammered, unable to look at her. Embarrassment, anger, and fear washed over him in an inseparable wave. *Jeezez, I could have hurt her. What the hell…? How long is this sorta' thing gonna' go on?* The nightmares had been coming for several weeks now. There had been none at first – just the deep dreamless sleep of exhaustion after the long tour. But now, the longer he was home, the worse it seemed to be getting. Sleep was no longer rest, but a gateway back to the chaos of Iraq.

"Okayyy", she replied slowly, massaging the red marks on her throat with one hand. "I'm sorry I startled you, hon."

"It's ok, it's ok," he stammered. " I was jest havin' a bad dream, and that's when ya' shook me; surprised me a little bit." He was still unable to meet her gaze. Silence hung in the air. She did not know what to say. Wanting to break the awkward moment, Warden swung his legs over the side of the bed and reached for his pants on the nearby chair.

"Do you…do you think maybe you should talk to someone 'bout these dreams?" she asked uncertainly.

Warden frowned as he buried the initial harsh response that was on his lips. "I'll be fine," he answered instead. "I had some dreams for a bit when I got home from Somalia, too. They went away. These will too."

She hesitated, wondering how far to push the conversation. "And what if they don't?" she asked gently to his back, as he moved away from her toward their bathroom.

"I dunno," he responded. "I'm not goin' to talk to any head-shrinker, if that's what you're suggestin'. I'll jest work it out. I always do."

"Gus,…" she began, trying to maintain some contact.

"I don't need anybody's help," he cut her off, shutting the door between them.

Chapter 9
The Promise

Warden slipped out of the house as soon as he had showered, still shaken by his reaction to the nightmare. He quickly got busy, spending the morning driving the fence line, searching for the spot where several of his cattle had escaped onto the neighboring spread. It wasn't hard to find: a large branch had fallen on the fence line in a storm two nights earlier, snapping off one of the wood posts. It took him less than an hour to dig it out and bury the new one, and re-string the wire. He felt satisfaction as he looked at his handiwork, particularly pleased at his ability to craft the fallen branch itself into the new support.

He had felt like a fool for a couple hours after his abrupt awakening, but the familiar feeling of working with his hands had settled him enough that he could now ponder what had happened. *If I can't separate memory from what's goin' on now, I'm in trouble,* he realized uncomfortably. *I might hurt Lil or even Amy. I can't let that happen. Or am I just overreactin'? It was just one incident, after all.* Weakly convincing himself that his reaction was an aberration, Warden returned to the house down the long dirt track leading in from the county road. Clint Black accompanied him on the scratchy AM signal from Lubbock. Warden could see Lil waiting for him on the covered porch that ran the length of their one-story ranch-style house.

He slowed as he neared the unpaved parking circle in front of the house so he wouldn't coat his wife with dust. Several chickens and an ancient farm cat scattered at his approach, and he stopped his truck in its habitual spot by the woodshop next to the house. He was hungry for lunch, his appetite returning after his earlier shaky start. He called to Lil as he lifted his tools from the truck bed. "Found it. A tree branch took a post down."

She didn't say anything until he stepped up onto the concrete porch landing, and then handed him a note. "Captain Smith called. They need you at the Reserve Center tomorrow: something about weapons," she said.

Warden could tell from her tight expression that she was not happy. She had been planning for the three of them to drive to church in Amarillo tomorrow morning and then go to lunch, and maybe even a matinee.

"Damnit," Warden breathed, looking at the familiar phone number on the slip. "I was hopin' to clear that brush out from behind the woodshop tomorrow. Now, I'll have to do that today, too."

Lil's frustration boiled over. "Why don't you just tell him you can't make it? That you've got plans."

Warden looked at his wife as if she had just spoken to him in Farsi. "I can't do that. You know that."

"Yeah, I know. You only just gave them an entire year of your life – and twenty two before that. God forbid you should take a full weekend for your family."

"Cap'n Smith wouldn't be calling if it was somethin' avoidable," Warden explained calmly, hoping to deflect the storm he could see gathering on his wife's face. "I know this is gettin' old. It's just there's a lot of housekeepin' to be done when a unit first gets back from deployment; equipment to square away – accountability issues and such."

"Gus, why don't you just get out?" she blurted, no longer able to contain the question that had been burning inside her since she picked him up at the airport. She regretted the words the moment she spoke them, and yet the force of her frustration spurred her on. "You've done more than your share. You've already got your twenty for your pension."

"Hmph," he replied, suddenly fascinated by the lines of dirt imbedded in his weathered palms. This was not a conversation he needed right now.

"Really," she suggested anxiously. "You were in Somalia, then Iraq. You spent two years on the East German border with the Cav regiment;

all that time up at Fort Drum. None of them were easy tours. Let someone else take a turn."

"Maybe," Warden said, but his brain knew that wasn't how it worked. *Ya' don't measure yourself against the lowest common denominator. Ya' measure yourself against…yourself.*

"Gus, what's there left to prove, anyway? You've done your part… and you have responsibilities here, too."

"Lil, what I've done isn't a big deal," he countered. "There's guys over there on their second rotation right now, counting Afghanistan. Some of these guys have spent two out of the past three years in the box."

"And that's *nuts,*" she argued. "How do you have a life with that sort of pace? Most of those troops are twenty, twenty-one years old. They don't have a wife and kids and a ranch to take care of. *They* aren't pushing forty-six," she added pointedly.

Warden winced at the mention of his age. He didn't think about getting older. He kept himself in shape through the physically demanding ranch work – running fence, chopping trees, lifting bales – all of it kept him lean and fit. The Army's physical training sessions on drill weekends were almost vacations from his daily ranch workout. He was always slightly amused at the middle-aged officers who congratulated each other on a "good workout" after several dozen push-ups and jogging a couple of easy miles. *Let's see 'em repair a hundred feet of washed out fence during a downpour,* he snorted, remembering just such an occasion a couple years earlier, when he had also ended up with a smashed thumb for his trouble.

But he knew that Lil had a point about age. He had noticed lately that strained muscles seemed to take longer to heal – and he was still limping slightly from where that calf had kicked him square on the shin last week. But age was not something he was ready to concede as limiting his daily activities.

"I know what you're saying," he replied, still not meeting her eyes as he walked to the water spigot at the end of the porch. He turned the handle and began to wash the grime from his hands, surprised by how cold the water was.

"But?" she called after him, recognizing he was just trying to placate her to sidestep the issue.

Warden worked the stinging cold water into his palms with his thumbs, watching the grime dissolve. "We're in the middle of a war," he answered.

"An unnecessary war…"

"That don't matter."

"My opinion doesn't matter? Thanks so much."

"That's not what I said…" he replied, his voice rising.

"Sounds like that's *exactly* what you said," she accused. Lil didn't understand why, but even this argument was providing a level of welcome contact with her husband that she had missed since his return home. *He's been so…flat since he got home. Even at the airport he was distracted…*

"Listen!" he ordered, turning back to face her. He instantly softened his tone as he saw her recoil from his "Army voice."

"Listen…please…" he said more softly. "It's not my job to decide whether it's a necessary or a stupid war or whatever. My job is to show up when and where I'm told, and to take care of my men. I don't have the luxury to decide whether it's worth my time or not. My job is to do what I'm told, and to try keepin' my people alive while doin' it. If I get all wrapped up in this pro-war, anti-war bullshit, it's just gonna' distract me from doin' my job well."

"So you don't care if the reason you get your head shot off makes sense or not?" she challenged, angry and wanting to fight. It was at least some form of emotional contact with her husband.

Warden didn't understand this side of his wife. *She just doesn't get it.*

"Keepin' my troops from getting' their heads shot off – whatever the reason – is what I care about. Trainin' and keepin' them alive is what I care about. Bullets don't have opinions and I can't afford to be thinkin' about the politics or anythin' else about this. People sittin' here at home have all the time in the world to argue 'bout that sort of nonsense. Soldiers don't. They can't."

"I know all that, Gus," she conceded. "I've been with you through sixteen years of your career. What I want you to think about is why does it always have to be *you?* Let someone else step up and do it for a change. There's no shame in leavin'. You've done your part."

My part..., that's the thing isn't it? How do I explain to her that ya' can't just walk away? Ya' don't recognize it when it happens, but if you stick 'round long enough you go from being in the Army to bein' **of** *the Army. I'm just another piece of equipment at this point. A bit beat up, but broke in well.* He looked at his crooked fingers, fractured countless times over the years on various field exercises or deployments. *Ya' don't walk away. Not in the middle of a war, leastways. Ya' stay until ya' get killed or too hurt to be of any good – or until they toss ya' out.*

Warden continued working the cool water into his palms with his thumbs, watching the grime flow toward the small drain set in a low spot in the concrete. *When had that happened? That change from bein' the young guy who was just goin' to do the Army for a few years to get some college money? I remember in Germany I was just doin' my time and plannin' to get out at the first opportunity. But then they made me a sergeant and it seemed to make sense to give it another tour. Even after I left active duty and went in the Reserves, I always felt like I could just walk away from it whenever I wanted. When did that change?*

He thought over his career. The water and the surrounding homestead faded.

"I can't wait to get out of this hellhole and hang up these boots," Hodge said through his gap-toothed smile as he loaded boxes into the back of the HMMWV. The morning sun of Mogadishu was already oppressive, causing his uniform to stick to his back. "No more 0500 wake-ups, no more first sergeants, and sure as hell no more Skinnies tryin' to light me up," he grinned.

"Yeah… yeah," a much younger Warden replied sarcastically. "You love this stuff. Where else can ya' get paid for handin' out soccer balls to kids?" He nodded toward the boxes his friend was loading into the truck bed. "Hell, back in the world people 'spect you to work for your paycheck," he teased.

Warden and Hodge had been in the same platoon in basic training several years ago. When Warden had gone off to join the 11th Armored Cavalry in West Germany, Hodge had done a couple of back-to-back rotations in Korea. They had now linked up again with the 10th Mountain Division detachment sent to help bring peace to the warring factions in Somalia. The fact that the type of peace each tribe in the conflict wanted was the complete extermination of its neighbors made the mission "an opportunity to excel," as they facetiously labeled any mission where the chance for success was slim from the start.

"Why don't ya' come along?" Hodge asked. " After we play Santa Claus…," he gestured toward the two big cartons containing soccer balls to be distributed to the local urchins as part of their 'hearts and minds' mission, "we're gonna' slip over to that Paki unit and see if we can trade them for souvenirs."

Warden was tempted at the chance to get outside the wire of their base camp and break up the monotony of deployed life, but replied, "Nah. Thanks, anyway. I gotta' get this damn correspondence course in if I ever want a chance at makin' E6."

"Suit yourself 'Sergeant Major,'" Hodge teased, flashing a grin as he secured the tailgate on the HMMWV. "I'll see you at chow."

The entire mission had been a setup. The local warlord's offer to facilitate the soccer ball giveaway had been interpreted as a positive breakthrough by the staff wonks at Division who did not understand the culture and were overeager to report any small success. They had prohibited heavy weapons in the convoy due to their desire to demonstrate their trust to the locals. The warlord wasn't as generous, and had placed two snipers in opposing buildings at the agreed-upon distribution site. It was his desire to create a deadly cross-fire and thereby demonstrate his strength by gunning down the overly trusting Americans.

Hodge's flak jacket had been inadequate to the task at this close range, merely serving to slow and only partially deflect the high-caliber round between his shoulder blades as he squatted before the smiling child with the outstretched arms. The saving grace, if any, was that the slight deflection kept the round from exiting Hodge's chest, saving the child's life. But Hodge was still dead before he hit the ground.

Later that night, Warden had intimidated the young medical clerk on duty to let him visit Hodge's body in the portable refrigeration unit being used as a morgue. Inside, the three bundled slabs looked identical in their dismal black wrappings. He only knew which Hodge was by reading the tags dangling from each body bag.

"Not so funny, now, huh, pardner?" he intoned in a low voice, not sure what to do now that he was there. He wanted to see Hodge to make sure this too was not just some colossal Army screw-up, but he didn't know if it was sacrilegious in some way to actually open the bag. He stood nervously rubbing his fingers together, his breath forming clouds of mist in the freezing air.

"Screw it," he declared, stepping forward to fumble with the metal fastener. A cloud of moisture escaped from the body bag as he opened it, liberating a freakish ethereal cloud to float above the body. It was Hodge: the Army hadn't gotten this one wrong. His friend's colorless features almost made him unrecognizable to Warden, who was used to seeing a grin on a healthy, tanned face.

"What'd ya' hafta' go and do this for, huh?" he spoke to his friend. "Now who am I gonna' shoot the shit with? McMillan? He's always rambling on 'bout his daughters and how smart and beautiful they are. Hell, you got the good end of this deal." He paused, waiting, although for what he didn't know. The stink of bitter chemicals filled his nostrils. He looked about the small 8-by-10 container with its lifeless inventory.

"I'm sorry," Warden began, as tears flowed unrestrained down his face. "I'm so damn sorry. I could've seen 'em – done sumthin'." He struggled to say more, but his throat had closed to a painful crack.

Wiping his nose on the hem of his T-shirt, Warden looked back into his friend's dead face. His voice cracking, he continued, "This ain't happenin' again, OK? I make you that promise. I will be there next time...every time, from now on. Don't you doubt it."

Hodge's silence hung like an accusation to Warden.

The cold was beginning to make Warden's forearms ache. He looked down at the icy clear water splashing onto them and splattering onto the cement of his porch. Water was on his face, as well, running onto his chin. He quickly wiped his face on his shirtsleeve before answering his wife's question.

"Look, next weekend's Amy's birthday. We'll take her to McDonald's and out to a movie, how's that?" he asked. "She still likes those happy meal things, right?" Turning around, he saw Lil was gone. *How long has she been gone?* The large puddle that had pooled about him and spilled off onto the grass suggested a disturbing answer. "Damn it," he said aloud, as he turned off the spigot.

Chapter 10
The Newbie

Captain Smith had summoned Warden to the Reserve Center because the unit's weapons shipment had arrived from Fort Bragg. As unit armorer, Warden was one of four with the access codes to open the arms vault and secure the weapons. The M16A2 rifles had been thoroughly stripped down and blasted free of a year's worth of grit and dust in giant high-pressure, mechanical cleaning vats at Fort Bragg before being returned to the unit. Warden's job was to check each weapon thoroughly to ensure all parts were present and then log them back into the unit's books by serial number. It was repetitive, mind-numbing work, but Warden took pleasure in the familiar feel of each rifle and the almost musical exchange of the bolt and receiver as he exercised each weapon.

"Sergeant?" a voice came from the entrance to the vault. Warden looked up to see one of the new privates who had joined the unit's stateside detachment while the rest of them had been in Iraq. He recognized the pale features and the red, close-cropped hair of the soldier, but couldn't recall his name. He did notice that the troop was at least twenty pounds overweight by Army standards. His rounded facial features were an obvious contrast to the sharp cheekbones that still characterized the Iraq vets.

"Yeah, Private, what can I do for you?" he replied, without interrupting his task.

"Lieutenant Colonel Barrus said I should find you and see if I can arrange to get qualified on the M16. I need it for promotion and while you were all deployed there was no range time for the rear detachment."

Warden looked about, irritated, at the numerous racks of weapons he still had to check. The assistant armorer, PFC Jamie, was supposed to be here helping him but had not reported for duty.

"Have you seen Private Jamie today, soldier?" Warden asked, ignoring the original question.

"No, Sergeant."

Warden pulled back the charging handle on the next rifle, looked to make sure the chamber was clear, and then worked the bolt back and forth. The dry rasping noise told him that the weapon needed some lubricant before it passed his inspection. *If I don't do it now, some knucklehead will take it out to the range, dry as a bone, and jam it on the second round,* he thought, having seen just such stupidity a dozen times throughout his career. *People treat these weapons like rental cars, 'stead of the onliest thing keepin' 'em alive downrange.*

"When's the last time ya' qualified, Private?" he asked, without looking up.

"Well,…um, I really haven't…uh…done that yet, Sergeant," the troop replied meekly, color coming into his pale cheeks.

Warden paused from his task and glared at the soldier. "You haven't range qualified on the M16 – *not ever?*" he asked incredulously.

"No, Sergeant."

"How the hell did you get out of Basic without qualifying on your weapon?" Warden challenged, his voice rising slightly.

"Well, I got sick the week we did our final weapons qualification – was in the hospital with chicken pox – and so I didn't finish that block of instruction."

"So why didn't they recycle ya' then?" Warden knew many troops who had had to take a second go-around in basic training to fulfill critical skills requirements.

"My drill sergeant said he was gonna' get me a waiver of some type, because it wasn't my fault, and they needed to graduate a certain number of recruits out of each class."

"That's bullshit, son. What they did was pencil whip it to graduate ya' so their numbers looked good." Warden felt his temper rising at the training detachment pushing through a soldier who had not even qualified on his weapon. "Did ya' lose a buncha' trainees from your class before this happened?"

"Uh…yeah…, umm, I mean, yes, Sergeant. It turned out a recruiter had covered up some drug charges on a whole bunch of guys out of Florida and someone talked, so six or seven guys were washed out of our company overnight."

"Nice. The DI's[15] didn't train ya' and the rear detachment didn't train ya', so now you're dumped on me, not knowin' which end of the rifle to point," Warden fumed. *This is the sort of crap that gets people killed when the balloon goes up.* Warden thought back to the day Major T had been hit and how Private Ridlin had popped an insurgent in the head on the run at 250 meters. *This kid would be more likely to accidentally shoot a squad-mate than to hit an enemy.* He reached for the tube of oil on the rack above him and squeezed some onto the bolt face and continued to work the action.

"I,…I want to do it the right way, Sergeant. I haven't had any say in this, you know? They tell me to stand there, I stand there. They say you've graduated, I say, 'OK, I've graduated.'" The young man's frustration was obvious in his voice.

Warden put the now lubricated rifle back into the weapons rack and secured the metal bar across the front with a heavy lock. He grabbed a rag from the open bin next to the field desk and began to wipe the oil from his fingers as he walked slowly toward the private standing in the doorway. The troop's nametag read "Connelly." Warden paused, his boot tips inches from the young soldier's. He could smell some type of cheap body spray on the young troop, which all these kids seemed to wear these days.

"All right, Connelly. Here's the deal. Number one – stop snivelin'. Right now you're worthless. A soldier who can't move, shoot, and communicate is just gonna' get hisself and those 'round him killed. So, I'm gonna' teach ya' to shoot."

"Thanks, Sergeant."

"Don't thank me, dough boy. It's my job. *Your* job is to lose ten damn pounds by the next drill. When you get yourself shot – and I promise you that will happen – I'm not luggin' your fat ass on my back to a medic."

"My family's always been a little heavy…" Connelly tried to explain conversationally.

"Bullshit!" Warden barked, cutting him off. "I don't care that your daddy was a fat-ass too. Stop shoving donuts and 'tato chips in your cake-hole and start running five miles a day. They may not have trained ya' in Basic, but your butt belongs to me now."

Connelly opened his mouth to reply, but no sound came out. He wasn't sure whether Warden hated him or not, but he did know that he had finally encountered someone who gave a damn and was going to make him perform. In a strange, twisted way it was almost refreshing.

As green as he was, the young troop recognized that Warden was someone to listen to, and maybe even be a little afraid of.

"Now get out of here," Warden said, dismissively.

"Yes, Sergeant!" Connelly replied in a strong voice and spun on his heel.

Warden watched the young soldier walk away. Connelly's shoulders were back and his stride was confident; not the casual amble of a civilian. *God, I love this job,* Warden thought.

Chapter 11

The Last Chance

Master Sergeant Winkle stuck his head into Colonel Burr's office. "Sir?" he wheezed.

"What is it, Winkle?" the POD growled impatiently from behind his desk without looking up.

"General Merdier on line 358, Sir."

What does that SOB want? Burr wondered, looking down at the flashing light on his phone. He paused, noticing that Winkle's head was still in the doorway. Burr glared at the darkened bulb on his inter-office intercom. Its malfunctioning required him to endure Winkle's personal presence whenever a call came in for him. "Get out," he snapped.

"Yes sir, I'll get right on that," Winkle offered meekly as he closed the door.

"Good morning, Sir. Nice to hear from you," Burr lied into the handset.

"Cut the crap, Burr. What are you trying to pull?" the one-star commander of Burr's higher headquarters accused.

"Sir, what do you…?" Burr started before being interrupted.

"Listen, choir boy: I know you're up to no good. I have a recommendation for a Silver Star – a *Goddamn Silver Star!* – staring me in the face, that *you* sent up."

"Yessir," replied the POD with feigned enthusiasm. "Sergeant First Class Warden. One of the most outstanding NCOs that I've…"

"Do you think I'm stupid, Colonel? Is that what you're telling me?" Merdier barked into Burr's ear. Burr winced. "You wouldn't throw a drowning man a rope unless there was an angle in it for you. You did my bidding for four years before I shipped you off, so I know what a sneaky piece of crap you are. Now spill it."

"Sir, we've had our differences in the past, I know," purred Burr. "But command has a way of changing a man. I'm sure you know that," he lied.

"Hmmph," General Merdier snorted into the phone, realizing that bullying Burr was not going to get him any answers. "Well, whatever your angle you've put me in a helluva' pickle as usual. Major General Oldhaus got wind of this somehow, and just got off the horn with me. Thinks it's a great idea. Is all for it! A fitting end to his tenure as USACAPOC commander…'a real feather in his cap!' he says."

The POD smiled widely. His leak of the award recommendation to Colonel Rabbit had worked just as he had hoped. Never one able to keep his mouth shut, Rabbit had immediately shared the information with his master, thereby eclipsing Merdier's ability to reject or downgrade the award without first consulting with the commander of all Civil Affairs forces. Manipulating Rabbit, and through him, his boss's boss, had never been easier.

"So my hands are tied, and I need to favorably chop on this and send it up." *Otherwise I'd put my shot at replacing Oldhaus at risk,* Merdier knew.

"Well, I'm sure Sergeant Warden will be very grateful for your support, Sir," Burr replied, still grinning at successfully outflanking Merdier.

"Look, Burr - you're a sneaky SOB, and you've maneuvered this pretty well. Impressively, even…" Merdier granted, a reluctant tone of admiration slipping into his voice.

"Sir…"

"Shut up and listen. You probably know already I have the inside track for Oldhaus's slot once he clears out. I can't afford for anything to screw that up, and neither can you."

"Me, Sir?" Burr replied, uncertainly.

"Yes, *you.* As much as it pains me to say this, the branch is not very deep with colonels that are ready to step up and pin on stars – especially in the middle of a shooting war. The days of just handing out commander coins and attending conventions went out the door when we stumbled into Iraq."

Burr felt his pulse begin to quicken.

"Anyway, you're about the only candidate out there who hasn't managed to step on himself somewhere along the line. Hermann had the inside track until the tech wonks in G6 found four gigs of porn on his hard drive during a routine upgrade – you mention that to *anyone* and I'll have you shot: not good PR."

"Yes, Sir," Burr replied, trying to sound sincere. *Hermann? Didn't think he had it in him.*

"The only other real candidate is Martin from the 804th."

Burr's breath caught in his throat at the sound of his rival's name.

"His unit did a pretty good job in Iraq, but the back alley gouge on him is that his executive officer held the unit together while Martin crawled inside a bottle the first time they took casualties."

Burr allowed himself to breathe again.

"So that leaves you and a handful of other weak sisters who have never deployed."

"It's very humbling to hear that, Sir."

"Don't bother with the bullshit, Colonel. I know you've been weaseling for a star since you landed in my lap at the 42nd. You've left a trail of bodies a mile high behind you. I never thought you stood a chance with all the enemies you've made, but here we are. Sometimes even the runt of the litter makes good, I suppose."

"Yes, Sir," Burr replied evenly, not sure whether to be offended or grateful, but smart enough not to provoke his boss.

"Anyway, I didn't call to be your damn career counselor. This whole medal thing is spinning a bit out of control and you need to know what a shit storm you've started. Oldhaus's brother works on the Hill and has some connections over in the E-Ring at the Pentagon. Wants to send his brother out in a blaze of glory and so he's lined up the Army Under-Secretary for Personnel and Manning to come pin this piece of tinsel on your boy: 'First Civil Affairs soldier to get the Silver Star,' and all that. They plan to make a big deal out of it in the press for recruiting purposes."

Burr's palms went damp. This *was* spinning up into something big.

"Here's the bottom line, Doug,…"

Burr was taken aback at Merdier's use of his first name. He'd worked for the General for five years in one capacity or another and had never been addressed as "Doug." It was either "Burr," "Colonel," or a colorful string of epithets, depending upon the General's mood.

"... you pull this off, and both you and I are set for the rest of our careers; me at CAPOC and you at the 42nd. You screw this up in the slightest, and you'll swing alone. Understand?"

"Yes, Sir, I do," Burr replied unevenly, the magnitude of what his plan had become suddenly beginning to worry him.

"Good. Then I only have one more question before I forward this with a favorable recommendation."

"Sir?"

"This is on the up-and-up, right? This whole damn thing is airtight, correct? Assassination attempt – Haji with a suicide belt – the whole nine yards? Because if it's got even the slightest smell to it someone is going down, and it's not going to be me."

Burr had added the embellishment about the suicide belt himself after Captain Smith's narrative had not seemed *compelling* enough. He licked his lips nervously in anticipation of his next words.

"Every word is gospel, Sir."

"All right, all right," Merdier murmured on the other end. "Well, get back to work then and quit wasting my time." *Click.* The line went dead.

Burr could feel his heart pounding as he set the receiver down. *Calm down, calm down,* he told himself, trying to breathe deeply. *Everyone has already agreed to send this through. Nothing will go wrong. We put together a little ceremony, pin the medal on that corncob, drink a few glasses of punch, and I get my star* and *dodge the next deployment.*

Burr felt his confidence returning. He pictured himself sitting in Merdier's big leather chair at Fort Rucker, his feet comfortably propped up on the walnut desktop, his aide bringing him a morning cup of coffee as he moved papers from the left side of his desk to the right.

That's what it's all about, he sighed.

Chapter 12
The Covenant

"Sir, can I have a word with you a second?" asked Warden as he poked his head into the brigade commander's doorway.

"Yes, Sergeant, what is it?" answered Colonel Burr, not looking up from the pile of papers before him. Inwardly he wondered if word had leaked to Warden regarding the proposed citation. *I'll fry Smith alive if he opened his mouth.* He also wondered where Winkle was – it was that worm's job to keep people away from him.

"Sir, I was wonderin' if we might be able to arrange some extra time at the firin' range for the new troops. Lieutenant Colonel Barrus said I should check with you, as you're plannin' on goin' over the trainin' schedule this weekend."

"Yes I am, Sergeant. I'm looking at it right now," Burr replied with a strained tone, still not raising his eyes.

"Yes, Sir," replied Warden, pausing to give the commander a moment.

Warden was unsure what to do with himself, as Burr continued to silently frown at the mass of paperwork on his desk. Knowing Burr's propensity toward formality, Warden slowly pulled himself into a position of "at ease" with his hands clasped behind his back. *At least it gives me something to do with my hands,* Warden thought as he linked them firmly together in the small of his back.

The clock behind the commander's desk ticked off a full two minutes before Burr came out of his trance. "Too aggressive," he announced to the room, slapping his hand upon the sheaf of documents before him. He raised his eyes and fixed them upon Warden for the first time, scrutinizing the NCOs weathered features.

Warden knew better than to ask any questions of Burr. The commander had made clear at his first formation that this unit was not going to be one where give-and-take was welcome. "Do what you're told and we'll get along fine," had been Burr's inspiring message to the troops of his new command.

"Too aggressive," repeated Burr. "Sergeant, I can see from this proposed training schedule that you were well-intentioned. But you have to remember we're not in the desert anymore. We don't have the luxury of a large wartime budget that we can spend at will. We're back under Reserve funding streams where they dole out their love by the thimble."

"Yes, Sir," replied Warden, waiting for his moment.

"The Army Reserve standard is one day at the firing range per year and that's what they budget, Sergeant. Where do you think the money is going to come from for this so called 'operational weapons training' you've proposed for the September drill?"

Seeing his opening, Warden dove in. "Sir, the first thing we learned when we got in the box was that troops who only fire once a year were no good under real combat conditions – dust in the weapons, unable to clear jams, not able to fire on the move. Heck, Sir, you remember those desert convoys? We trained for years here at home firin' from nice fixed concrete foxholes at stationary targets. It took about five minutes in Iraq to learn how useless that was when we had to fire left-handed from HMMWV's bouncin' along the highway at targets we could barely see."

"Yes, Sergeant; I was there if you recall," Burr said slowly and somewhat impatiently. Both men knew that Burr had spent the greater part of his war in the air conditioned headquarters on Camp Babylon – not on convoys. "I recall the…challenges that we *all* faced. However, my question is not whether the training is desirable in a perfect world, but how we would get more live ammunition when we're only allotted enough for one standard qualification round."

"I was thinkin' 'bout that, Sir. I see on the trainin' schedule that there's some VIP event on the third Saturday in September that we're putting a lot of discretionary funds into. If we could trim that back a bit and allocate those resources to the extra weapons training, we could do it. Enough for the enlisted to get some live-fire experience while moving, anyways. I've already called in a favor from a buddy at Range

Control, and getting a firing range is not a problem. We just need to get the ammo and our bodies down there."

Burr cocked his head as he looked at his enthusiastic underling before responding. "I can see you've put a lot of thought into this, Sergeant – and while I admire your...*energy*, it's not possible. 'Trimming this event back,' as you state it, is not possible. This is no ordinary 'glad-handing' session. I've pulled some very delicate strings to get the Army Under-Secretary for Personnel to visit our unit and make a special presentation. This visit is critical to the future of this unit." *Not to mention* my *future,* Burr thought.

"Sir, all that political stuff is way beyond my pay grade. What about if I just take the newest troops – the ones who've never deployed yet? There's this new private – Connelly – hasn't ever qualified. That'd be no more than a half-dozen total. Six troops wouldn't be missed."

"Sergeant, it is exactly the new troops who need to be exposed to an event like this. It helps build morale and unit cohesion for us to be recognized this way. A man of your experience should recognize that."

"Sir, from m*y experience* the best way to build unit cohesion is stayin' alive the first five minutes after Haji lights us up. Goin' to some party won't do that."

Burr could feel the vein in his left temple begin to pulse. "Sergeant," he began slowly, keeping his rising anger in check, "I am trying to give you the benefit of the doubt here, and your motives are admirable. But you are correct – it *is* above your pay grade to set the priorities for this unit." Although his natural temptation to simply berate the

NCO into a state of subservience was instinctive to Burr, something in Warden's manner told him that that wouldn't work this time. "That job is mine, as coincidence would have it," he coolly continued, "and I have decided that this event will not be altered in *any* way. *Everyone* will be there, and everyone will participate. Am I clear?"

Warden had years of practice maintaining an impassive exterior, having endured a parade of weak or self-interested commanders over the years. Inwardly his guts were twisting. *We haven't learned a Goddamn thing,* he thought. *We sent a buncha' minimally trained troops off to Iraq who had more training on "courtesy to others" than they did on their assigned weapon. We were lucky we were up against an enemy more interested in runnin' away than fightin', or a lotta' those troops down in the drill hall might not be here. I thought it would be different when we got back. I'm a damn fool.* "Yes, Sir," was his unconvinced response.

Recognizing he had won another round, Burr now moved to consolidate his position. "Sergeant Warden, as unlikely as it is that this unit will deploy again for another three or four years," he lied, "I, too, recognize the importance of maximizing weapons familiarization." The POD exuded warmth and sincerity as he spun his web. "Let me make you this pledge. If we can pull off this ceremony in September with the full aplomb that I know this unit is capable of, you have my personal commitment that during annual training next summer we will dedicate an entire week of field training to tactical scenarios and weapons skills." *The fact that this unit will be back in Iraq by then and I'll be wearing a star at Fort Rucker is beside the point,* he smirked inwardly. "How does that sound?" he smiled encouragingly at the NCO.

"That would be great, Sir!" Warden found himself blurting, to his own surprise.

"Fine…fine," said the POD as he rose and came around the corner of his desk extending his hand. "We have an understanding then."

Warden saw his own hand reach out and instinctively return the offered handshake. As his rough palm met the soft, smooth flesh of Burr's, he resisted the temptation to pull back. He could not help feeling that he had been maneuvered into an unholy alliance that he didn't understand. The POD's half-smile, the flat reptilian eyes – he had seen it all before in the desert, and it never bode well for the recipient.

"Well, that'll be all then, Sergeant," concluded Burr as he took Warden by the elbow and steered him to the door. "I'll send taskers to you through Lieutenant Colonel Barrus to get the new troops up to speed on drill and ceremony. I want an honor guard worthy of Arlington when the Under-Secretary gets here. This will be a dress greens event, and so you need to make sure each man has the appropriate uniform. And for God's sake check their ribbons to make sure they have all the ones they've earned. No screw-ups. Spit and polish will be the rule of the day."

"Yes, Sir," Warden replied in an uncertain tone, wondering how it was he had come to request additional weapons training and was now leaving in charge of a fashion show.

Chapter 13
The Battleground

"Hon, why don't you grab a table while I get the food?" suggested Lillian Warden to her husband.

"OK," said Warden, leading his daughter by the hand to one of the plastic booths in the front corner of the dining room. He slid around to the back of the table so that his back was to the wall. A children's play area, consisting of a small pit of brightly colored plastic balls, was to his right against the wall. *Can't be seen from the street unless I lean forward*, he thought, testing his range of vision out the large plate glass windows. Old habits were hard to break, even in the bright colors and forced cheer of McDonald's.

"Daddy, can I go play in the ball pit?" his daughter asked, snuggling up to him in her best persuasive manner.

Warden continued to assess the room; *four kids and a couple moms in the back. Guy coming in the near side door and heading for the latrine; truck driver, maybe,* he concluded, eyeing the large leather wallet chained to his belt. *No bulge under his T-shirt. He's OK.*

"Daddy?"

"Hmm, what's that, darlin'?"

"Daddy, can I go play in the balls?"

"Umm, sure, hon; just don't get out of sight from me, OK?" *Don't know who's in the latrine already; haven't checked that,* he thought uncomfortably.

"OK, daddy," she smiled as she slid out of the booth and skipped joyously to the tiny play area. Massive fast food restaurant play areas had yet to arrive in Amarillo.

Warden followed her with a smile on his rugged face. *She's getting so big – looks more like her mother all the time.*

Warden took in the bright, plastic universe surrounding him. The smell of greasy fries filled the air. *The height of American culture,* he quietly chuckled to himself, happy to have an entire day to spend with his family. He remembered seeing a McDonald's in the distance from the highway during their trip from Kuwait City Airport to Camp Commando a year ago. *Can't imagine why a three thousand year old culture wants to import McDonald's. 'Course, it's better'n goat meat,* he admitted.

The side door on the far side of the restaurant opened and a teenage boy sauntered in. *A kid – uniform top – must be reporting to work. Nothing unusual,* Warden assessed subconsciously.

His stomach rumbled deeply. *Man, they're taking forever. I thought this was supposed to be "fast food."* Lil looked over at him from the counter where she patiently waited, giving a half-smile of boredom and a roll of her eyes to express her own impatience at the delay.

The side door opened again. Warden tensed as the jolt of adrenalin shot through his system. A portly woman in a traditional Arab burkah entered the restaurant, followed by two young men. *What the hell?* The woman had a slight limp and a dusky, round face framed by her black head scarf.

Warden felt himself begin to sweat. *She's a got a big damn bag over her right shoulder.* His eyes flicked to the right, where his daughter was throwing a plastic ball into the air and catching it. He looked back. His wife seemed unaware of the threat, her back turned slightly away from the newcomers. The men were dressed in blue jeans and short sleeve, plaid shirts. *Nothing in their hands – but they're moving away from the woman.* Warden flicked his gaze to the side door in the near wall, fifteen yards away, where the Wardens had entered the restaurant. *Nobody there; that's our way out if this goes bad,* he decided.

Lil looked at her husband from across the restaurant and sensed something was wrong; he had that *hard* look on his face she had seen before. *His body's rigid, and he's gripping the table edge.* She had never gotten totally used to the military side of her husband's personality, but he was usually pretty good at leaving it at the door when he came home – or at least he used to be. *Something is definitely causing him to shift gears now, though*, she realized.

He pointed to his eyes with his index and middle finger and then to her left. She smiled as she recognized the military hand signals. His use of them on family vacations was a running joke. "We are not your troops," she would good-naturedly rebuke him on those occasions. "Stay alert, stay alive," was his tongue-in-cheek retort, as they maneuvered their way through dense crowds at Disneyland or Six Flags.

She could sense something different today, however. She began to mouth "what?" to him, but was interrupted. "Ma'am, here's your order," offered a bespectacled teenager from the other side of the shiny metal counter. "Sorry for the wait."

"Oh…, oh, thank you," Lil replied, turning uncertainly to accept the tray.

They're moving to the front of the restaurant. Warden followed the men with his eyes. *The woman is at the counter. Why are they splitting up? This is no good. We're outta' here.*

Quickly rising, he moved toward his daughter. The two young men were gesturing in an animated fashion at each other across the table they had just settled into. The Iraqi woman was at the other cash register. *That bag has something big in the bottom*, Warden noted. *Goddamnit! Why doesn't Lil look? She saw my signal. What's a Haji doin' in Amarillo? Whatever – I don't care; we're movin' – now!*

"Amy, we're leavin'," he addressed his daughter briskly.

The child looked up surprised and then perturbed. "I don't wanna' go, daddy. I just started playin', and I'm hungry."

"We'll play somewhere else, honey. C'mon, we need to go. Now." His voice rose in insistence as she failed to move.

"No!" Amy declared. "I wanna' play! Where's mommy?"

"No time. Were movin' – let's go." He reached down and grabbed the little girl's upper arm.

"Nooo!" the girl screeched in a high voice. "You're hurting me!" her voice rose in displeasure, as she pulled away to free herself from his grip.

Warden released her thin arm and looked over at the counter where his wife was watching him with a furrowed brow. *Goddamn it! She's going into that bag,* Warden noted as the Haji woman, standing at the next register, unshouldered one of the straps of the large purse. *This is it!*

Lifeless eyes stared up into his. Her eyebrows and lashes had burned away. He felt anger rising in himself. She was smiling. The corners of her mouth were twisted back in a twisted grin, revealing a half dozen brown teeth behind blackened lips. Smiling.

"Lil!" He called across the restaurant. "Leaving!" Warden scooped his daughter up, tucking her kicking body next to his right side, as he bolted for the side door. Measuring the short distance in his mind he calculated that a medium sized charge would take them both out unless he got a solid wall between them and the blast. Fifteen feet… ten…five; he was out the door. The writhing package under his arm was still shrieking, but he paid no attention. Warden rapidly moved toward the back of the building where their truck was parked and the restaurant's brick construction would protect them. He glanced behind himself to see Lil just emerging from the restaurant. *Hurry*, he urged her inwardly, his heart pounding.

Warden opened the truck's passenger side door and tossed Amy into the cab, closing the door while she continued her tantrum.

"What *are* you doing?" Lil questioned as she approached from the restaurant. "Our food is still in there. What is going on between the two of you?" Lil looked into the cab where Amy was kicking her small feet against the dashboard.

Warden was silent, still tensed for the imminent blast. *She's not gonna' understand. She doesn't have a mind for this sort of thing.*

"Well?"

"Look, I got a bad feelin' in there. Somethin' was goin' down, and I needed to get us out of there."

Lil looked at her husband, confused and scared at the stress on his face. His eyes were still darting about, looking for something. She glanced back at the restaurant where a carload of teenagers had just pulled up to the drive-thru speaker. Turning back toward her husband, she carefully asked, "Gus, what do you think was *going down*? I only saw a kid's birthday party and Mrs. Aziz with her two boys."

Warden remained silent for a moment, sorting his wife's words. "Who the hell's Mrs. Aziz?" he asked in an irritated tone. "And since when are there any Iraqis in Amarillo?"

"Her husband is an engineer at the granary – and I think they're Jordanian, by the way. They moved here from Houston while you were away."

"Oh, that's beautiful," Warden blurted. "I can't wait to get away from that rat hole over there and now the damn Hajis are right here waitin' for me. What's next, a Goddamn mosque?"

Lil stared, not sure what to say. She knew her husband was not exactly open-minded on many things, but she had never heard him seriously use such hateful, sweeping statements about people before. He had always told her that he didn't care about the race, religion or anything else about a person so long as they had your back "when something went south." This was totally out of character.

"You've changed, Gus. What the hell did they do to you over there?"

"Hmmph," Warden grunted, averting his eyes. He had not told his wife of any of his close calls in Iraq, other than a veiled reference to being "nearby" when Major T had got hurt. "Let's just go, huh?" he replied, trying to move past her.

"No, I mean it. Talk to me!" she demanded, grabbing his arm. "That *show* in there wasn't from the same guy I sent away to Iraq."

"No kidding?" he answered sarcastically, knowing that the old Warden had disappeared in Iraq a long time ago.

"So, what's the deal?" Lil continued. "Is this intense, humorless guy thing a permanent fixture or can we look forward to putting it away soon? You used to be pretty good natured – funny even – remember?"

"I remember," he replied, still avoiding her eyes, as she refused to release his arm.

"So what's going on? Talk to me," she insisted again.

"Look!" he barked, turning to face her. She recoiled slightly, to Warden's embarrassment. He softened his tone slightly before continuing. "Look, you need to understand sumthin'. I spent every moment of the past twelve months deciding whether I was gonna' hafta' kill each person I encountered or whether they were gonna' kill me. Men, kids, old women – it didn't matter. The bad guys used everyone to get to us. I had to size 'em up to see if they was wearing a bomb belt or packin' a weapon. Did they look nervous? What were their hands doing? Were they signaling someone with their actions? Was a kid trying to distract me, so his cousin on a rooftop a block away could put a 7.62 slug in the back of my head?" He paused, feeling his pulse racing and his voice rising.

"But you said you weren't 'in it' like in Somalia. You said it was more like charity work and helping the Iraqis get their government back together."

"There, uh…were a couple bad times…I didn't write 'bout all of it. Didn't want to worry ya' none."

"So what really happened over there?"

Warden took a deep breath. *How can I possibly explain somethin' that still makes no sense even to me?* "It was complete anarchy, Lil; even worse than Somalia. No front, no uniformed enemy, everyone a potential enemy. A Haji wants to work with ya' one day, and the next day wants to kill ya', cause somebody else is gonna' kill his family if he doesn't. Kids were sellin' whiskey and porno to the troops one day, and then gettin' paid off to drop a grenade in their HMMWV the next. Old women smugglin' rifles and explosives under their clothes. It takes a little piece outta' ya' every time ya' meet one of those people, cause ya' might end up havin' to kill 'em. Ya' make the wrong decision and some Haji kid grows up with no father, or hesitate at the wrong moment, and your entire team comes home in a bag."

Warden looked down at his hands, which were shaking. Lil pretended not to notice, heartsick at her husband's anguish. He pushed them into the back pockets of his jeans and stared down at his boot tips. "So, multiply that by the several thousand of 'em I dealt with over there and this is what's left. Each time chipped away a little piece of that 'good nature,' as you put it, and replaced it with pure, cold survival. I can't turn it off. I've tried, but I can't turn it off any more."

Lil Warden had never considered herself much of an "Army wife." She didn't buy into the old "white glove" scene where the spouses of the higher ranking NCOs and officers held sway over the more junior soldiers' wives. She had simply been there for her husband throughout his Army career, because she recognized its importance to him, and so tolerated the baggage that came with being married to a soldier. She knew that the Army, despite its representations to the contrary, was not tolerant of anyone operating below 100 percent. This caused many troops to cover up injuries or problems they were having. But she also knew that her husband was in over his head this time. "Gus, I really think you need to go talk to someone…"

"We've been over that," he snapped. "Everyone's been through it. I'm not anythin' special. Just give me some space, OK? Everything will be fine if ya' just stop naggin' me," he lashed out defensively.

The verbal slap made her pause, her mouth opening and closing several times without sound. Warden was oblivious to the hurtful impact of his statement, as he struggled to insulate himself from further discussion.

"Let's just go," he directed, pulling away and walking around to the driver's side door.

Lil looked in the window of the truck to where their daughter lay quieter now, crying softly. *I'm scared,* she realized. *I don't know what to do or if anything can be done. Maybe I'm just making it worse by asking him these questions.*

"Let's go," Warden ordered again, as he settled into his seat.

Lil climbed into the truck, gently moving Amy onto her lap. Lil fought back the tears that she knew would irritate her husband further. *I just don't know what to do,* she thought helplessly.

Chapter 14
The Diner

Warden had driven by Ike's Diner out near Route 40 and the railroad tracks a hundred times, but had never stopped, always rushing to or from some other commitment. Today he had nowhere to go – no place to be. He had slipped out of the house early that morning to avoid continuing yesterday's discussion from the McDonald's with his wife. He and Lil had barely spoken the rest of that day, although he could feel her concerned glances on him several times. *Just what I need – pity,* he thought, resentfully. This morning his 1994 Chevy pick-up seemed to turn itself into the gravel parking lot of the diner on its own.

How have things gotten so screwed up? he wondered as he sat staring at his hands gripping the steering wheel. *Life was gonna' be so good once I got home. I told myself I wasn't gonna' get worked up over little stuff anymore. Was gonna' spend more time on the 'portant things – Amy,*

Lil. Now it's all going down the crapper. Nobody needs a half crazy ex-infantryman hangin' around. Why can't I shake this?

Warden stepped out of his truck and slammed the door. He caught his reflection in the door's window. *Lookin' damn old,* he thought as the dark bags under his eyes were apparent even in the glass. *Who's behind those eyes, anyhow? Not sure I know anymore.*

Pulling away from the disappointing visage, he walked to the front door of the diner, where a rickety screen door with torn mesh was off its hinges, propped in front of the gumball machines in the narrow entrance. Warden walked past the door into the main dining room – such as it was. Across from the entryway a long lunch counter with stools ran the length of the room, while orange vinyl booths were set along the front wall to his left and right. *Empty,* he noted, looking about. *Good.* Warden ambled down to the far right end of the diner and slid into the last booth. He rubbed his tired eyes with the palms of his hands, his mind still tired from the confrontation with his wife and another sleepless night.

"Mornin' hon," the cheerful voice announced at his side. "Can I get ya' a cup of coffee?"

Warden let the palms of his hands slip down from his face to look into the fresh, youthful face of the waitress. She had blue eyes set in a pretty, thin face. Her dark brown hair was pulled up in a bun at the back of her head – one long wisp tracing the outline of her right cheek. The plastic tag on her blouse announced her name as "Monica." *22, maybe 23 tops,* thought Warden. *Pretty. No concealed weapons,* he morosely joked to himself. "Yes'm," he replied, "Some coffee'd hit the spot 'bout now."

"Be right back" she smiled and turned, the close trim of the orange server's outfit revealing an athletic build as she returned back behind the counter. Something in the way she moved caught Warden's attention, as she glided her way to the coffee station.

The harsh blast of a horn in front of the diner jerked Warden's attention back out through the large front windows, where a white pickup truck had accidentally pulled in front of an oncoming SUV. Warden could see the panic on the pickup driver's face, as the Ford Explorer's screeching brakes locked to miss him.

"Aammbusshh!" Mantis' voice cried in slow motion, as Warden's helmet cracked off the windshield. Warden turned his neck painfully to see the small white truck blocking their path, as the Iraqis in the front threw open their doors and came rushing out. As Warden's feet made contact with the pavement, movement toward the rear caught his attention, as the Iraqi burst from behind the trailer. He has something in his hand …detonator?! On his right, the brigade commander struggled vainly to get free from his seat belt. Involuntarily, as if he had suddenly stepped outside himself, Warden saw the M16A2 rifle raise in his hands, the stock snug into his shoulder, and his cheek press against the side of the weapon.

Crack! "Oops, I'm sorry," the waitress giggled as she dropped the saucer and cup a bit too heavily upon the Formica table top.

"Wha…?" Warden exclaimed, surprised by the clatter of dishes and the sudden close proximity of the waitress.

"I'm sorry, sugar," the young server apologized with a smile. "Didn't mean to startle ya'."

Warden's vision was momentarily blurred as he tried to focus back in on his surroundings. Two trails of moisture traced down his cheeks.

"Hey, are you OK?" the girl inquired gently, concern filling her voice.

Warden brought the palms of his hands up and pushed the moisture to the corners of his eyes. His hands shook slightly as he pulled them away. *I'm a damn soup sandwich,* he thought.

"Yeah, uhm, I'm fine. Thanks," he answered, clearing his throat. "My mind was just somewhere else for a minute."

"No problem," the girl replied kindly. "How 'bout I get ya' some pie to go with that coffee?" she offered. "My treat?"

Warden raised his eyes to the girls face again. Kindness was written in her eyes. The pursed lips betrayed her slight nervousness.

Great; now I'm a charity case, Warden realized, his embarrassment growing from blubbering like a damn recruit. *Free pie for the crazy bastard from Iraq.*

"I 'preciate it, ma'am. But I'm fine – really. Just need to be alone a bit."

"Alright, but if ya' wanna' talk, ya' just let me know, OK?"

Warden nodded, without responding, wishing that she would leave. He looked down into the half-filled cup of coffee. *I used to lead men in combat, and now I'm a pity party for a waitress. It don't get much lower than this.*

"Cause I've learned that keeping things inside is a sure way to eat yourself alive, ya' know?" she continued, still looking at her customer with concern.

Her ongoing concern was more than Warden could bear this morning. "Look, what's it to ya' anyway?" he lashed out angrily. "I'm just some damned stranger in off of the street. Just leave me alone, OK?"

"No problem," she replied quietly, seeing the pain centered between his eyes. "I didn't mean to intrude. You just remind me of someone."

"Yeah, who's that?" he challenged, expecting a line about an old boyfriend or even her dad.

"Me."

Warden snorted audibly, taken off guard by her answer. "Darlin', we couldn't be more different, trust me…"

"No really, I…"

"Bullshit!" he involuntarily blurted,   "Look, hon – ya' seem like a nice young lady, but you and me ain't got nuthin' in common." *Go away,* he thought.

"Why?" she replied, bristling and not retreating an inch. "Cause I slop coffee for a living? That means we're so different?"

What the hell is goin' on here? Warden asked himself. *I sit down, and I get coffee. Isn't that how it's supposed to work?*

"Look, I'm sure you're a real nice person and all that, but I don't need nobody takin' care of me, OK? I've got things under control." He began to slide toward the edge of his seat. *I need to get outta' here.*

"Marine?" she challenged, still not backing off.

Warden looked at her blankly, shocked into silence. "Look…" was all he could get out.

"I'd say you're a Marine," she continued. "Which means Iraq."

Warden felt his anger rising at being psychoanalyzed by this stranger. "Listen, Goddamn it," he burst forth angrily, slamming his right hand on the table. "I don't wanna' talk 'bout the war. I don't want to hear how Goddamn much you admire me for my service, and I certainly don't wanna' tell some Goddamn *waitress* how I'm feelin' right now, OK?" It felt good to Warden to release some of his frustrations, but he surprised even himself at the intensity of his explosion.

"Sure thing, Sergeant," the girl replied evenly, not shrinking a bit from his outburst. She met his angry gaze without blinking – her eyes locked onto his. They glared for what seemed like minutes, as only seconds passed. Tentatively she reached down with her right hand

and gripped a few inches above the hem of her mid-calf length skirt. Warden watched her, puzzled.

This is getting' real damn weird, he thought, looking about for anyone else in the empty restaurant. Slowly, she pulled the hem of her skirt upward several inches, until it rose above where her knee should have been. The strap that held the prosthetic limb to what was left of her leg dug tightly into the stump several inches above her knee. Red, scarred flesh flashed angrily as the fluorescent lights of the diner reflected off of her wound. Tears welled in her eyes, as they flashed angrily.

"We have nothing in common, right?" she challenged Warden. He was unable to speak – his mouth hung open slightly. He stared at her wound, wanting to look away. *How had that...?* He forced his eyes away from her tortured flesh and raised them to her face, which was now streaming with defiant tears.

Unable to maintain her stare any longer, she turned away, head held high, and strode the practiced gait that had first attracted Warden's attention back behind the counter.

Warden looked after her as she reached the middle of the counter and turned her back to him. She grabbed an unseen object and busied herself with scrubbing it furiously. He could see anger in the red flush running up the back of her neck and the vigorous motion she made while scouring the object. *How did she know I was a sergeant?* he wondered. *I've never seen her before. She got the Marine bit wrong, but...who...what the hell?*

"Aw, shit," he said aloud as he stood up from his seat. *I need to get outta' here.* He opened his wallet to pay and found he had only a $5 bill. *This day can't get no better,* he concluded. He pulled the bill out and tossed it on the table, before heading to the door. He paused momentarily before exiting, his hand upon the frame inside the shabby front door. He could hear the girl still giving a workout to the object in front of her.

"Sorry, ma'am," he said to his shoe tops and walked out into the cool morning.

Chapter 15

The Collector

Warden rapped his knuckles on the trailer's front door.

Two or three seconds passed before the door swung open a few inches and the round, pleasant face of Mrs. Jamie appeared. "Oh, good morning, Sergeant Warden," she smiled. Her son Tyler had been in Warden's platoon since graduating from his advanced training two years earlier. All of the unit members were well known to each other's families in Amarillo. "Tyler is out back, working on his car." His mother was the only person that Private First Class Jamie tolerated calling him by his Christian name; in the unit he was just "Jamie."

"Thank you, ma'am," Warden replied, removing his worn ranch hat. "I'll just go round and speak to him for a spell if ya' don't mind."

"You go right ahead. Can I bring you something to drink? Lemonade?"

"No thanks, ma'am. I 'preciate it though. You have a good day now," he said, backing politely away from the door.

Warden followed the well-worn path through the sparse grass around the side of the double-wide. He set his face into business mode as he approached the clanging and swearing issuing from the single-car garage some yards behind the trailer.

Inside, Jamie was up to his elbows in dirt and grease as he leaned inside the hood of his '92 Nova. "Mice!? Who the hell ever heard of mice livin' in a car engine?" he declared angrily to the world at large. The young troop was amazed that a year sitting up on blocks had turned his wheels into a home for wayward rodents.

"Jamie," Warden said as he entered the open door of the small pole building.

Lifting his head out of the engine compartment Jamie returned an easy, if somewhat grease-smudged smile. "Hey, Sergeant Warden, howareya'?"

"I'm great. You're not. Ya' missed drill last weekend."

"Ohh…yeah, yeah. I meant to call. Guess I forgot. Been real busy round here since I got back, ya' know? Lookin' for a job; gettin' the car rollin' again."

Warden frowned. "Jamie, this ain't a social club. It's the Army. Ya' don't just show up when ya' can fit it in." By virtue of their service together in Iraq and his respect for Jamie's weapons skills, Warden gave the young soldier more leeway in their conversations than he would to other subordinates.

Jamie pulled himself completely from under the hood, looking around for something to clean his dirty hands upon. "Yeah, I know, Sergeant," he said, reaching for a torn T-shirt laying across the top of a three-foot square cardboard shipping box. "Time just got away from me. In the Sand every day was Groundhog Day, ya' know? I've been havin' some trouble getting back in the swing of things here."

Warden's eyes flicked to the now uncovered cardboard box. It was three quarters' full of yellow, camouflage and flag-colored "ribbon" magnets – the type people plastered onto the backs of their cars. He stepped over to the container for a closer look. Inside, hundreds – maybe even thousands – of "Support the Troops" ribbons and other pseudo-patriotic magnets were jumbled over each other. "What's this?" Warden snorted, as he gestured toward the box.

"Ribbons. I've been collectin' 'em."

"Collectin'?"

"Yeah. You know the big Wal Mart? I go out there and collect them; take 'em off cars." Jamie replied matter-of-factly, still wiping his hands.

Warden paused, watching Jamie calmly wipe the excess grime onto the old brown T-shirt. "Why?" he asked.

"Well, they're for the troops right? So people can show their appreciation?"

"Yeah. So?"

"So, I figure if they're for the troops, and I'm a troop, then it's OK to take 'em." Jamie grinned and tossed the now filthy shirt back onto the box.

"Uh-huh," Warden grunted, watching Jamie closely. He had never known Jamie to step out of line even slightly before their deployment. His reliability was one of the reasons Warden had made him assistant armorer for the unit.

"I mean, it made these people feel like they were doing somethin' good when they bought those things, right? So it's like a favor I do them, ya' know? Now they can go buy another one and feel good all over again 'bout supporting the war."

"Yer' nuts – ya' know that, right?" Warden stated matter-of-factly.

"I'm nuts?" Jamie repeated, crinkling his brows as he considered the statement.

"Yeah. Certifiable."

"Because I want people to feel they're contributing to the war effort?"

"Because ya' bother to do it at all. Period."

"Well I don't see it that way, I guess."

"No kiddin'."

"I provide a valuable service," defended Jamie piously.

"Service?"

"Yes, Sergeant. I allow people to express their love of our country by buying these ribbons again and again. If I didn't do it….well, how would they show that?…I mean you can only put so many ribbons on one car."

"But ya' *steal* 'em."

"It says right on 'em, 'Support the Troops.' I'm a troop."

"Jamie, what the hell would ya' do if someone caught ya'?"

"Oh, they have."

"They *have*?"

"Oh yeah, a few times."

"What happened?"

"Well, the first time I felt kinda' embarrassed. So I told the guy I was an Iraq vet and the ribbon upset me 'cause it reminded me of all the bad things from the war."

"Did it?"

"Nah, but what was I supposed to say: 'I'm doin' you a favor?' People never understand when you're tryin' to help them," Jamie lamented.

"What'd the guy say?"

"He apologized to me and said he admired me for my service."

"He apologized – to *you*?" Warden asked incredulously.

"Yep," Jamie beamed proudly.

"You were stealing the ribbon off *his* car, and he apologized to *you*?" Warden asked again.

"Uh-huh. He was very sincere; said he'd be honored if I kept his ribbon."

"So… what'd ya' do?"

"I accepted his apology and left."

"With the ribbon?"

"Of course; it proved my point: It made him feel good. I couldn't deny him that. It would be selfish. He had the pleasure of buyin' that ribbon, and then he had the pleasure of apologizin'. Now he'll enjoy buyin' another new one – it's like a patriotic hat trick."

Warden had no idea what a "hat trick" was and just stared at the young soldier in disbelief. Jamie did not seem the least bit self-conscious. "How'd others react?" Warden probed.

"Oh, 'bout the same. Sometimes I tell them I was so moved by their display that I couldn't contain myself. They like that one. Sometimes I tell them I became a pedophile because of the combat stress and can't help myself."

"Pedophile?"

"Yeah – you know – someone who can't help stealing."

"That's a '*kleptomaniac*,' you moron; a pedophile is a kiddy-diddler!"

"Ohh…," Jamie replied slowly, looking at the dirt under his fingernails. "Well that explains the reaction that lady with the little boy gave me. I wondered why she offered me money to go away."

Warden looked Jamie over. *Is he just pullin' my leg?* he wondered. *Never really known Jamie to be a joker; not the sharpest stick in the pack, but a straight arrow.*

"What are you going to do with all of these?" Warden asked, again gesturing to the box.

"The ribbons?"

"Yeah, ya' gotta' have about five hundred in here."

"One thousand, three hundred and eight," Jamie corrected.

"Whatever. What're ya' gonna' do with them all?"

Jamie paused and looked seriously at Warden for a moment. "Do you really want to know?" he asked seriously.

"Yeah."

Jamie looked about a second and then poked his head outside the garage to make sure no one was listening. "It's a secret, so you can't tell anyone, OK?"

"Believe me, I'm not tellin' anyone 'bout this," Warden replied sincerely.

"Well, OK. I'm gonna' make a memorial."

"A *memorial.* To what?"

"To all those who sacrifice so much for this country."

"The troops?"

"No...no, the people who bought the ribbons."

"You're going to build a memorial to the people who bought the ribbons?"

"Uh huh," Jamie grinned. "Absolutely."

"Yer' nuts."

"I thought we covered that already," Jamie laughed.

"Some things bear repeatin'," Warden replied in his gravelly voice.

"No, really, Sergeant. I have a place picked out down by the creek, near the old Korean War Memorial. I'm going to lay them all out in the shape of a really giant ribbon and call it the 'Memorial to the Second Great Patriotic War.'"

"Ya' think the town's really gonna' let ya' do that?"

"If anyone tries to stop me I'll accuse them of not supporting the troops. No one wants that label."

"And ya' think that'll make a difference?"

"Who would you support – a combat veteran with one thousand, three hundred and eight pieces of blessed patriotic magnetism, or a ribbon-hating bureaucrat?"

"Hmmm, ya' may have a point there."

"Darn right I do," Jamie declared triumphantly.

"Whatever. Look – what you do on your civilian time is none of my business. Just don't get tossed in jail and make sure to get your backside to drill next month, ya' hear? I got better things to do than keepin' your fat out of the fryer with Colonel Burr."

"OK, Sergeant. Wilco," replied Jamie.

Warden turned and walked slowly back toward the trailer. *Guess I'm not the only one who left somethin' over there,* he mulled.

Chapter 16
The Step

Warden tried to forget about the waitress all during the following week, busying himself with the accounts for the ranch and reviewing projections for the upcoming year. Yet every time he let his mind wander, he saw the young woman standing in the diner aisle, her wound exposed and defiance on her face.

There were several ways for him to get about town for the usual staples and ranch supplies, but he frequently found himself driving past the diner on Route 40, glancing through its big windows. The parking lot was often at least half-full. It had not been busy the Monday morning when he had been there last, and so it was two weeks later he found himself driving past *Ike's* on another Monday morning, on his way to pick up some grain for the horses.

One car in the lot, he observed, easing up on the gas. *Ah, what does it matter?* he asked himself. *She'll have forgotten all about it; written me off as a crank.* He continued on to the feed store. There, as he hefted the fifty-pound sacks of grain from the loading platform into the truck bed he convinced himself that he just needed to let the episode go. A week earlier the mare had been spooked by a black snake in her stall, and she had kicked out some boards. *Gotta' get home and fix that,* he told himself. So when his truck pulled into the gravel parking lot and turned itself off in front of the diner, he muttered a low "damnit" under his breath.

Taking a deep breath, Warden got out of the cab and approached the entrance. Someone had reattached the screen door to its frame in a makeshift way; it stood open, held in place by a latch hook. Warden poked his head inside the restaurant.

She was there, standing on a rickety wood chair with her back to the door, writing the day's specials on a chalkboard above the kitchen's serving window. An older black man sat at the far left end of the counter, hunched protectively over a bowl of soup.

"Morning, Sergeant," she said brightly, without looking around. On the board she finished writing, "Meatloaf with Mashed Potatoes - $4.95."

"Mornin' ma'am," Warden replied, trying to not sound surprised that she knew it was him. He went down to the far right end of the counter, as she stepped down off of her perch. "Well, looks like you boys are gonna' give me my exercise today!" she declared in a cheerful voice, smiling as she glanced at the twenty empty counter seats between her two customers. The old man to her right looked up momentarily and grinned before returning to his bowl.

Embarrassed, Warden said, "I can move if that's easier for you ma'am," quickly rising from the circular stool.

"Sit yourself down," she directed with a motion of her hand, as she glided toward him, pad in hand. "And it's 'Monica' from now on. *Ma'am* is for first time guests." There was no anger or awkwardness from their last encounter in her voice. "So what can I get you, Sergeant?"

"'Gus.' *Sergeant* is for first time guests," he replied with a weak smile.

"Stop the presses," she teased, looking about in feigned shock. "This man has a sense of humor."

Warden fought unsuccessfully not to smile at her antics.

"So, what'll it be, Gus? I still have that two-week old piece of pie saved for ya' in the back," she smiled, her eyes crinkling with amusement.

Warden took a deep breath and looked down at the counter, before raising his eyes to her again. "First, I wanna' 'pologize for bein' a horse's ass when I was in here last time. I had kind of a rough day and was feelin' sorry for myself..."

"...and then those two cars nearly crashing out front took you back *there*, didn't it?" she finished.

"Ma'am…Monica, you're lucky this ain't the Middle Ages or they'd be burnin' you as a witch," he chuckled. "How'd ya' know things like that? Like how'd ya' know just now that it was me coming in here?"

"The second one was easy," she laughed gently: "Your old heap out there needs a tune-up so bad that it has its own special dance-cadence goin' on when you pull up out front."

"OK, you got me there," he admitted.

"The first one was only a little harder. Only time I seen a Texan with a thousand yard stare and water runnin' down his face like that was in Iraq. Bravo Company, 511th Quartermasters – fuel handlers."

Warden tilted his head slightly, as he assessed this new information. *The posture, the confidence in her look…Yeah, she just might be…*, he thought.

"Specialist Monica Gonzales," she offered, sticking out her slender hand for Warden to shake.

"Where at?" he responded returning her firm grip.

"Fuel Point Dragoon – near Talil."

"Yer' kiddin' me? I've been to Dragoon… on the MSR16 on the way north to Hillah."

"Before or after it blew up?" she asked, the smile fading from her face.

"Aaah…must've been before…," he pondered, thinking back to the dusty refueling point with its few scattered tents and several lines of refueling trailers next to supply route *Tampa*. "Early April '03."

"Yeah, well that was a couple weeks before it happened. They never found out exactly *what* happened – leastways they never told me. It wasn't real bad duty. We thought we were kinda' lucky really, even though we were in the middle of nowhere. Nobody was shootin' at us, and we had tents and cots – unlike a lotta' the troops, sleepin' in holes in the ground."

Warden nodded, remembering the 1st Marine Division troops in their chemical warfare suits, laying in what looked like pre-dug graves during a short pause in their advance on Baghdad.

"One night the whole thing just went sky high," Monica recalled. "Some people thought it was Fedayeen[17] – others suspected it was somebody smokin' in an area with a leak. Twelve fuel trailers went up that night, and we lost seven people. I was lucky – big old piece of trailer came right through the side of our tent and clipped this one off right below the knee." She patted her right leg gently. "Same piece hit my friend, Sheri. They told me later in the hospital that she never knew what hit her. That's good, I suppose," her voice trailed off, as she looked out the large front windows for a moment.

Warden waited.

"So, three months and six operations later they told me they couldn't save the knee because of all the infection, and so they made a clean start up above. So here I am," she declared, spreading her arms wide, an unconvincing smile on her lips.

Warden knew there was nothing he could say at this moment that would not sound either forced or maudlin, so he simply nodded. He had dealt with other wounded combat vets and knew that not being treated any differently was what they wanted most.

"Anyway, that's the long way 'round the mountain to how I knew who you were," she concluded. "Last time I saw eyes like yours it was my team sergeant, Sergeant Perez, bending over me as they loaded me into a Black Hawk to evacuate me to the CSH[18]."

"Hah!" she laughed, suddenly recalling the moment, one year and half a world away. "Know what he said to me, as they loaded me in?"

Warden shook his head, as he watched a genuine smile creep across her face.

"He said I should quit lying around and get back to work," she laughed, tears of amusement filling her eyes.

Warden chuckled appreciatively, knowing well the NCO technique of never letting troops give in to feelings of despair. Without thinking, Warden suddenly reached across the counter and gently took Monica's hand into his own large grasp, giving her palm a reassuring squeeze. She returned the pressure with her left hand, as she looked upward and wiped her eyes with the back of her right hand. Warden was shocked to see her small hand in his own on the counter. Embarrassed, he quickly released it and withdrew his large forearm back across the counter. *What am I doing?* he wondered.

"How 'bout a slab of that nasty, two-week old pie, Specialist?" he asked, trying to lighten the mood.

"Comin' right up," she replied cheerfully, her red rimmed eyes regaining their customary sparkle.

"And, uh, Monica?" he began, as she hesitated to look back to him.

"Yes?"

"I ain't no damn Jarhead. Army – E7."

"Well, you missed your calling," she teased over her shoulder, as she moved away with practiced tread to place his order.

Over the following weeks Warden found himself at the feed and hardware stores near the diner more often, for extra nails, medicine for the calves, rat traps – there was always something else he needed. Lil put his frequent trips down to mere restlessness. His errands seemed to coincide with periods of increased stress, such as when the news detailed the increasing number of US casualties in Iraq. Warden didn't consciously plan these trips; he just knew that a few moments at the diner gave him a momentary lift in his otherwise grey existence.

A couple of weeks after Monica told him about Fuel Point Dragoon, a powerful car bomb rocked downtown Al Hillah – his old stomping grounds in central Iraq. Warden watched the television coverage of burning cars and screaming civilians late into the night, frustrated that he could not reach out and take control of the situation on his screen. He showed up at the diner two days later, while running an errand to get salt licks for the cattle. This time he did not come empty handed.

Monica was behind the counter filling sugar dispensers as he clumsily made his way through the front door, his arms full. "Hey, watcha' got there?" she greeted him, as he struggled with his awkward load.

"Oh, it's nuthin'" he said, his cheeks a bit flushed. "I had these steps layin' round my workshop and thought ya' might find a use for 'em." He held out the sturdy, three-step platform in front of himself for her inspection.

"Now what possible use could I have for that?" she said with a chuckle, looking over her shoulder at the specials chalkboard on the wall above.

Warden half smiled and turned a deep shade of red. "Give it a try," he encouraged, stepping forward and passing the steps to her over the counter.

Monica took the steps, noticing the fresh smell of wood stain and a few tell-tale curls of newly shaved wood beneath the top step. "They're beautiful," she said as she admired the workmanship, including the extra heavy duty bolts for sturdiness. "Thank you," she added softly.

Warden simply nodded, avoiding eye contact as he sat down at the counter.

Monica placed the steps down and gave them a try, stepping up and down briskly several times. Even with all her weight on the topmost step, the assembly was as solid as the floor beneath.

"I figgered a six inch rise on each step would be about right for ya'," Warden commented as she tested her gift.

She was about to wisecrack, "While they just happened to be laying about your workshop?" but caught herself, knowing that it must have taken Warden a lot of sand to make this for her. "They're perfect," she replied instead.

"Hey, Ike!" she called through the metal-framed window into the gloom of the kitchen. "Look at me!" she bragged as she went up and down the steps.

"Nnnggh," a deep voice replied. Warden knew of Ike – the cook – but in all the weeks he had been stopping by the diner, he had yet to actually see the reclusive character that made the pies Monica was forever pushing on him.

"That's high praise coming from Ike," she teased coming back up to the counter. "Well, thank you again, Sergeant."

"Gus," Warden reminded her, looking up from the one page, handwritten menu.

"Alright, Gus," she answered, "One good turn deserves another. The pie is on me today. What can I get you?"

"I'll just have coffee, if ya' don't mind. I've been gettin' fat on all this civilian food." He refrained from adding that his meals at the diner on top of Lil's cooking might have something to do with it as well.

"Hmm," she replied, with feigned seriousness and knotted brows. "It's not every hombre who gets free pie from me, ya' know."

Concerned that he had just insulted her again, Warden quickly replied, "I…I'd love some pie – I jest ate, though, and it wouldn't set right."

Monica laughed through fingers clasped over her mouth. "Don't worry 'bout it, Gus. I was just teasing you."

"Oh…well…I didn't wanna' seem ungrateful," he offered. *I'll never understand women,* he thought.

"You don't joke 'round much, do you?" she asked with a smile, her eyes searching his tanned face. She could sense something was going on with him today.

"Not so much anymore," he replied somberly.

"So, how're things at your unit? Everyone settling back in?" she asked, trying to pick a neutral subject.

"Yep. Everyone's settling back in; just like we never went. Training schedule's a joke – full of lectures and touchy-feely classes. No tactical training."

"Well, maybe they're just trying to ease you back into the routine," she suggested.

"Maybe," he replied, blowing on the steaming coffee she set before him. "But I don't think so. The commander is a pencil-pusher with a check-the-block mentality – just like before the war. Doesn't seem to realize we need to get this new crop of troops up to speed and keep an edge on the old ones."

"Well, you just got back. It'll be years before you have to go again, won't it?"

"Hmmph," Warden snorted. "Not a chance. SECDEF is still operatin' under some fantasy that a half-dozen SF¹⁹ guys on horseback can win any war with enough gizmos and gadgets to back 'em up. He wants to re-fight Afghanistan over and over so him and his boys aren't plannin' for the numbers that are gonna' be needed to hold Iraq together. Not to mention the next war in Shitheadistan – wherever that may be. We'll be back in the box within eighteen months, tops: crappy equipment and untrained kids still comin' home in bags – nuthin' ever changes."

She watched the cloud come over his face as he bared his concerns. "Do they have good pie in Shitheadistan?" she asked quietly, trying to mask a smile.

Warden screwed his face up as he pondered her question. "Hmmm, good point. I'll have a slice of the peach."

Chapter 17
The Confidant

"Padre?" Warden asked, sticking his head into the small office at the end of the hallway that ran the length of the Reserve Center.

"Hey, Sergeant Warden, you lost?" Chaplain Clay joked, looking up from the book on his cheap metal government desk. In the desert Warden had not been much of a church goer. Even when Clay's Sunday morning services had been the only break in the monotony of the "every-day's-the-same" existence of a deployed unit, Warden had spent those extra hours cleaning his weapon or checking the vehicles for the next mission.

"It's about Jamie, if ya' got a minute?" Warden answered, uncomfortably.

"Sure, sure, come on in," the Chaplain invited, gesturing toward one of the brown metal folding chairs across from him.

Warden sat down, observing the Chaplain a moment before beginning. Clay had a reputation in the brigade for being easy to talk to and for caring about the troops. He had spent as much time outside the wire in Iraq as any soldier, and had won quite a few converts because of his willingness to go where the troops went. That and his unabashed devotion to fine Cuban cigars: the troops felt that a man with a vice of his own was someone they could trust. The Sergeant Major described him as, "a man I could have a drink with on Saturday, and be proud to be buried by on Sunday."

"I'm worried 'bout Jamie, Padre," Warden began.

"What's going on?" Clay asked, leaning forward across the desk.

"He...uh, hasn't been quite...*right* since we got back. He missed drill last month, and when I went to talk to him 'bout it, I found he'd been doin' some other goofy stuff. He was solid as a rock in Iraq – best SAW gunner we had – but now he's flakin' off. I'm tempted to just lock his heels and give him a good reamin', but somethin's not right and I'm not sure how to 'proach it. I thought maybe you could kinda'...look into it."

"Did Jamie tell you what's bothering him?"

"Some gibberish 'bout helpin' people by stealin' their car magnets; didn't make any damn sense to me. I'm a platoon sergeant, not a social worker."

"Well, normally I wouldn't be able to tell you anything he and I had discussed," the officer began, "but the Command and JAG are already involved in this, so it's no secret. Do you remember Jamie's fiancé? That cute little girl from McLean?"

"Sure, she was at the going away ceremony, cryin' her eyes out."

"Well, they were getting married as soon as Jamie came home, so of course he trusted her. Gave her a general power of attorney so she could look after his things and …"

Warden knew what was coming before Clay could finish his sentence from the look on the chaplain's face. Any soldier who had been around long enough had heard horror stories of some poor troop who came home from war to find both his apartment and bank account empty because a young wife or fiancé got tired of waiting and had a piece of paper that let her clean him out, *legally*.

"She wiped him out," Warden stated, finishing the Clay's sentence.

"Yep – bank accounts, belongings, *everything*. And ran up several thousand dollars on his credit cards…all of which he's legally responsible for since he voluntarily gave her the papers," concluded Clay.

"Damn…," Warden groaned, rolling his eyes toward the ceiling.

"Word is she found some new young sucker over at Fort Sill and moved up there," Clay added.

"Has someone contacted the police?"

"Captain Smith made a call, but they said there's no crime. Jamie gave her the papers of his own free will. It's immoral, but not illegal."

"Damn…," Warden repeated, shaking his head.

"That's why he's back living with his mom right now. Only thing he has to his name is an old car that his fiancée couldn't get 'cause it was up on blocks."

"What can I do?"

"Not much, I'm afraid. Just maybe cut him a little slack for a couple months while he tries to piece things back together. The war took a little bit out of all of us, but with Jamie it took his fiancée and everything he owned on top of anything else. He'll bounce back, but he may not find his same old self for a bit."

Findin' his same old self. There's a lot of that goin' round, Warden thought.

"OK, Padre, I 'preciate the intel," stated Warden, standing to leave. He turned and placed his hand on the doorknob, then hesitated. Turning back, he said, "Padre, mind if I ask ya' somethin' else?"

"Sure thing."

"I've noticed that there's guys who went over there who came back like it was no big deal – that it was just a year's break away from the old home-front grind; and then there's guys like Jamie who came back, well, *different.* I can't figure out how that can be true in the same unit with troops that basically went through the same things together."

Clay thought for a moment before speaking. "Well, I'm no psychologist and everyone has different levels of tolerance to stress," he began. "What bothers one person may just be shrugged off by the next. There's no accounting for that. But is it really true what you said – that everyone had the same experience?"

"Well, we were all in the same place together," Warden replied.

"Yes, but think about it. Most of the unit hardly ever went off the base camp, except to go to the Haji market to buy roast chicken or souvenirs – there were only a few dozen of you who were regularly running missions – dodging IEDs, seeing the impact of the war on a daily basis."

"Ridlin was with us most of the time through all that," Warden countered. "He seems fine."

The Chaplain chuckled. "Well, just between you and me, Sergeant Warden, I don't think Ridlin would know it if someone hit him with a bat. There's somethin' missing in that boy," Clay grinned.

"Maybe," Warden conceded. "What about Mantis? He seems OK, while Jamie is all goofed up."

"If I recall, Mantis wasn't with you the day Major Trevanathan got hit, was he?"

"No, he wasn't."

"Well, that was a pretty big event and makes a difference, right there. I'm a strong believer that making the conscious decision to kill another man changes you. Whether or not you hit what you're shooting at, the "no shit" decision to kill another man puts you into a different category of humanity. Seeing one of your close friends or team mates get hit badly often does the same thing. War is no longer an abstract 'CNN moment.' It's damn personal and different people react differently to that change."

"I still don't get it though, Sir. These troops were trained for years to be ready to pull that trigger."

"Sergeant, a lot of people don't know this, but I was enlisted before I went back to school and went into the Chaplain business. I've been to my share of field exercises and even took a brief 'vacation' to Panama with the 82nd[20] when we cleaned out Noriega. I don't care how many times you go to the qualification range or field exercises, the first time you put that rifle sight on another human being with real intent to shoot, it changes you."

Warden nodded, recalling one master sergeant early in the war who had to be sent back to the States for psychiatric treatment after their convoy had been sniped at on the highway. The guy had been in the Reserves for twenty years, and the first time he had to fire his weapon for real, his world came down like a house of cards. He hadn't even hit anything. Warden had been disgusted with the man's weakness at the time, but his own recent experiences gave him reason to question that condemnation.

"Jamie was in that firefight outside Al Salaam – killed one of those insurgents trying to flank you, didn't he?" Clay continued. "As we say in my business, you 'carry the mark of Cain' after that – knowing you've taken another man's life. That's a helluva burden for some to bear. Some care; some just shrug it off. Jamie might be one of those who can't get his head around that yet."

"Well, that's all above my pay grade, Chaplain," Warden replied haltingly, as the image of the dead Iraqi truck driver flashed before him. "Thanks for your time." He turned back to the door, suddenly uncomfortable that the Chaplain's remarks were hitting so close to the mark.

"And how are things in your world, Sergeant Warden?" Chaplain Clay asked, his eyes narrowing slightly as he observed the NCO.

"Couldn't be better, Padre. Just another beautiful Army day," Warden grinned sheepishly and ducked out of the office before anyone else tried to open his head.

Chapter 18
The Shield

Warden walked out of the bathroom, still wiping stray dabs of shaving cream from his ears with a towel. He had stayed up until 3 AM, watching news reports of the violent Shiite militia uprisings in Karbala and Najaf. Vicious urban combat between Muqtada al-Sadr's thugs and US troops was happening in the massive Najaf cemetery that Warden knew well. CNN's real-time images had worked him into a knot all night until several shots of Uncle Jack had anaesthetized him in his armchair.

We should've taken that bastard Sadr out when we had the chance, he thought. *The 1ˢᵗ Marine Division had been poised to do just that a year ago, but the mission was called off at the last minute by the State Department lackeys in the Green Zone, who feared "aggressive action" would destroy the stability in southern Iraq. Last night a bunch of young troops paid for that 'stability',* Warden mulled angrily.

He found Lil in the kitchen, cooking breakfast and listening to the radio.

"…has been ruled an accident by the local district attorney. The name is being withheld at this time," the announcer finished his story.

"Mornin', Lil," Warden greeted her blearily.

"Mornin'. Did you hear that?" she replied, turning off the radio. "There was a shooting accident over in Canyon. One brother shot another while out hunting. How horrible."

"Yeah, that's too bad," Warden offered nonchalantly. "I'm runnin' into town this morning for some roofing staples."

"The dead boy is fourteen," she offered again.

"I *said* that's too bad," he repeated.

"That's only ten miles from here, Gus. We may know those people."

"Lil, I can't get all teary eyes over some radio report; sorry."

"Nobody's saying 'get all teary eyed,' Gus. The slightest *real* expression of concern would be a nice touch, though."

"Hmmph. Got any coffee?" he asked.

"A boy's dead…in our community… and your concern is coffee?"

"Lil, I don't mean to be a jerk. But there's a lot of bad stuff in the world, and I can't be gettin' all sniffly every time some knucklehead screws up."

"But these are just kids…"

"*Kids* that age are carryin' rifles and fightin' wars all over this planet. Maybe I should just piss myself silly 'bout them, too?" he countered, regretting his words the moment he uttered them. *How do I tell her I could stick a knife in my leg these days and not feel it, without soundin' like some kinda' psychopath? I don't have anything left for "shock the community"-type news reports.*

"What's your problem this morning?" Lil asked, turning back to the stove.

"I just have no patience with morons anymore, if that's a *problem*. People are careless and then act surprised when something bad happens. Drive through town and see people not watchin' their kids playin' out on the sidewalk. If one of 'em runs out between two parked cars and gets run over they'll cry, 'Oh, how could God let this happen to me?' Not, 'how could I be such a lazy dumb shit by not watchin' my kid?' No one takes responsibility anymore."

Lil was silent.

Warden continued. "The margin between bein' alive and bein' dead is razor thin every day. The sheep just don't see it."

"The sheep?"

"Two types of folks in this world, Lil – sheep and guard dogs. The sheep blunder through life not 'spectin' anything bad to happen and then look shocked when somethin' grabs them by the throat."

"And you're a guard dog, is that it?" Lil asked with mild sarcasm.

"I am now."

"And bein' a *guard dog* means you can't feel any sympathy for a young boy who is dead and his brother who'll have to live with that guilt for the rest of his life?"

"Lil, I just don't have the emotion to spare for bein' used. The papers put that sort of stuff in there every day and on the radio to make you feel bad, so they can sell newspapers or air time. Vicarious sympathy; I don't like bein' manipulated. "

"Gus, do you really want to live your life with all of that armor on? You used to care about things – about people."

"I remember. I used to not see dead kids and old people layin' in the street too," Warden recalled. His thoughts drifted back to walking through the rubble of Al Salaam after two Cobra gunships had leveled the village so that his team could escape the ambush just outside Camp Babylon. The villagers had been held hostage by the insurgents so they could not tip off the Americans, and were buried beneath the mosque's rubble when the rockets struck. The frail limbs of children protruded at gruesome angles from beneath the fallen masonry. The brains of one old man had burst from his head and sprayed across a wide area when a large cinder block had crushed his skull. *Let that stuff get to ya', and you'll be paralyzed,* Warden thought.

"I know you saw a lot of bad stuff, Gus" Lil replied, wiping her hands on her apron. "So, how do I get the old Gus back? Remember when you left? You were realistic about the danger over there, but you also talked about maybe doing some good for those people when the shooting stopped."

"The shooting never stopped, did it?" Warden observed. "It's funny, ya' know?" he continued. "Ya' wanna' help those people, and ya' wanna' kill 'em at the same time. Ya' put yourself out there to make a difference every day, and they don't give a damn. I've seen way too many good guys lead with their heart and come home in a sack. Ya' turn one way, and there's some teenage kid where ya' think – *if we made a difference here he could have a decent life* – and then at the same time you know this kid is sellin' your every movement to the enemy for a few dinars. Ya' get back to your hooch that night when it's all quiet, and you're tryin' to drift off; ya' thank God you didn't have to shoot anyone that day. Next morning you get up and start thinkin' *'Anybody screws with us today and we'll waste 'em.'* Every Goddamn day is a roller coaster like that. It grinds ya' down 'til there ain't much left but dust."

Lil felt some relief that her husband was actually speaking to her about his experience for a change, even though the words were painful to hear. She resolved to keep him talking as long as she could. "You said there were good things though too," she added. "That little boy who pulled your major out of the destroyed HMMWV…"

"Yeah, that kid had a pair." Warden's eyes gleamed momentarily before becoming flat again. "But ya' can't let your guard down, 'cause the shit always hits the fan whenever you're not expectin' it. It never fails. When you're all locked and cocked and on edge waiting for the Hajis to hit you, nuthin' happens. Taking a convoy through the worst parts of Iraq – waitin' for an IED – waitin' for the ambush – there's *nuthin'*. Ya' spend a four-hour round-trip to Baghdad waitin' to catch one in the head, or for one of your buddy's vehicles to go up in a fireball, and when nuthin' happens you wonder if maybe you were overreactin'. Ya' start thinkin', 'maybe it's not that bad, ya know? Maybe I'm just wrapped a little too tight and need to relax?' And then the second – the *Goddamn* second ya' let your guard down, some crazy Haji bastard forces ya' to kill 'em. It's like a big, never-ending mind game."

"I'm sorry…"

"Nuthin' to be sorry about. It's my job." Warden felt he had said too much. He didn't want to be going down this road with Lil. *No need to burden her with it; won't do any good anyway, 'cept make her upset.* He reached out and grabbed his hat off the peg near the door. "I'm gonna' go check on the mare."

The porch door slammed behind him, leaving Lil alone.

"I know it's your job. And this is your family…" she said to the empty doorway.

Amy walked into the kitchen, attracted by the smell of frying eggs. "Where's Daddy?" she asked sleepily.

"I think he's still in Iraq," Lil said quietly. "He needs to find his way home."

Chapter 19
The Cave

The following month Jamie's place in formation was empty again. Warden's phone messages all weekend to Jamie's mother's house went unanswered. *I'm gonna' kick his butt,* Warden resolved the following Monday morning, as he dressed for the day. He had hoped that Jamie would run the arms room on Saturday and Sunday, while he drilled the honor guard for the upcoming VIP visit. Instead, he had been saddled with both tasks, leaving him in a foul mood which had not been improved by the fact that Ridlin had been detailed to the honor guard. Ridlin's involvement ensured that Warden had to explain every detail two or three times more than should have been necessary.

"Lil, I'm gonna' run into town and check on Jamie. You need anything?" Warden asked as he headed for the front door.

"I don't think so. Just be home by dinner. The neighbors are coming over."

"*Neighbors?*" Warden asked, warily.

"Yeah, I thought you should meet the Aziz family and see that they don't really walk around in bomb vests. They're coming over at six," Lil replied evenly.

"Jeezus Christ, Lil! Ya' gotta' be kiddin' me!" Warden roared in protest.

"Yeah, I asked them if they'd bring their Imam, too, and some of their friends from the Mosque. We're gonna' cook a goat in the back yard and do the call for prayer."

"OK, funny lady," countered Warden, feeling foolish at falling for his wife's trap.

"They *are* nice people. But actually, it's the Morrows who are coming over," Lil clarified, smiling at her own joke.

Warden visibly relaxed. He and Lil had known Bob and Wendy Morrow for years. Bob had been an explosive and ordnance disposal officer during the first Gulf War and now did similar work for the Amarillo Police department. The Morrows were the sort of company you could relax around and toss back a couple beers with, without caring that you had holes in your socks.

"All right, I'll be back in time," Warden promised as the door shut behind him.

Jamie's mother told Warden that he had just missed her son, who had gone out to "pick up some items." *That kid gets himself busted rippin' off those car magnets and I'm gonna' skin 'em,* Warden thought as he drove home. But it was with little surprise that he found his truck steering itself over to the diner. This was happening more and more frequently these days, and while he didn't want to admit it out loud, he knew that greasy spoon was one of the few places he ever felt like himself any more.

Warden walked up the two wooden steps and pulled open the screen door of the diner. *Still needs a paint job,* he observed, noting the curls of faded blue paint clinging to the frame. Behind him, a pick-up truck driving past honked. Warden turned to see a hand waving in his direction, but could not make out the driver.

As he stepped inside, the screen door crashed into the frame inches behind his head. Warden jumped and sweat burst forth from every pore of his body. He looked about embarrassed, but there was no one around to see his startled reaction. He turned to examine the door and discovered that someone had disconnected the air cylinder that had half-heartedly softened its closing for weeks. The broken operating rod hung from its bracket, but Warden did not forgive it for finally wearing out. *Goddamn door!* he cursed silently.

Peering back through the small service window into the kitchen, he saw movement. "Monica, you here?" he called.

Ike, the scruffy fry cook who according to Monica did not have a single clean T-shirt in his wardrobe, popped his face into the opening and peered out. "She's in the can," he tossed back gruffly, a cigarette butt locked between his lips. "What can I getya'?"

"Uh,...just coffee, thanks."

Warden had never actually spoken to Ike before. The cook had been an almost mythical figure, lurking in the recesses of the kitchen, his existence confirmed only by the occasional glimpse of a hairy arm in the window, and the guttural announcement, "Order up."

Moments later Ike waddled out the metal door from his lair, a saucer and cup balanced in his right hand, and Warden got his first good look at the man. The cook was balding and maybe 5 feet 4 inches on a good day, and Warden saw that Monica had not exaggerated about his clothes. Warden considered that he could probably describe the diner's entire menu just from examining the various stains on the cook's soiled apron.

Ike placed the cup on the counter between them with all the care of a pile driver, spilling a quarter of it into the saucer. He peered at Warden from under heavy lidded eyes. "You that Army fella'?" he asked.

"Uh, yeah, I suppose I am," said Warden, sitting down on the other side of the counter.

"Yeah... she talks 'bout you a lot," Ike offered.

Warden felt uncomfortable. *What'd she be talkin' about me with this…guy?* His discomfort grew as Ike stood staring at him.

"I was in," Ike offered, suddenly.

"Hmm?" Warden replied absently, looking toward the restrooms, hoping Monica would appear.

"Army. 25th Division – 'Nam."

Warden looked at Ike closely for the first time. Sure enough, the unit patch of the 25th Infantry Division was tattooed on the cook's hairy right shoulder. Fifty extra pounds and a three-day beard effectively camouflaged any other sign that a soldier hid behind the dirty apron.

"What branch?" Warden inquired, suddenly finding something in common with the kitchen dweller.

"11 Bravo – Infantry," Ike replied. "I was a tunnel rat."

"No shit?" Warden asked, his interest now piqued. "Tunnel rat" was the nickname for soldiers small enough to crawl into the underground labyrinth the Viet Cong had carved underneath South Vietnam, in which they concealed their movements, headquarters and supplies. Usually armed with just a 45-caliber pistol, a tunnel rat operated alone in a terrifying world of booby traps, enemy soldiers and the ever-present threat of being buried alive. If a tunnel rat was wounded, he was out of reach of any help; he would just bleed to death, alone, in a pre-dug grave.

"Yeah," Ike replied flatly, eyeing Warden closely. "Monica said you were in some shit."

"Little bit," Warden admitted. "Nuthin' like you, though. Don't know how you did it: I couldn't."

"Nobody can. You just do it anyway," Ike observed, shifting the cigarette butt to the other side of his mouth.

A silence fell between the two men. Warden reached over and grabbed a packet of whitener to add to his coffee.

"She's not feelin' too good today," Ike said.

Warden looked up. "Yeah?"

"Leg's botherin' her. All inflamed, she said. Somethin' 'bout the socket not fitting properly anymore."

"Is she goin' to the doctor?" Warden asked, concerned.

"Yeah, but they can't get her in over at VA for a few weeks, so…"

"That's crap," Warden interrupted. "She shouldn't have to wait that long."

"Yeah," Ike replied. "I told her to go home, said I'd cover for her, but she wouldn't. She's tryin' to save up money to reenroll in her hygienist's program. She dropped out 'cause of money."

Warden pressed his lips tightly together, anger ranging through him. *She never complains. I should get out of here. If I stick around she's gonna' feel the need to act like it ain't botherin' her.*

Ike continued to stand across the counter, looking at Warden. Again, silence fell across the two men. Warden was about to stand up to leave when Ike blurted, "You wanna' see something?"

"Uh, sure…," Warden replied uncertainly, taken by surprise.

Ike reached inside his apron and produced a fat wallet. He quickly opened it and pulled out a yellowed photograph, which he laid on the counter. "That's my squad," he blurted, excitement creeping into his voice. Five youthful faces in fatigues looked at Warden from their seats on a large mound of earth.

"That's me, second from the left," Ike pointed out. Warden squinted: the young Ike looked like a stiff wind would blow him away. The same heavy eyelids confirmed that it was the same person, though. A wide smile covered the youthful face.

"We'd just got a 72-hour pass for cleanin' out a rabbit warren full of Charlie[21]. See…see that guy on my right?"

"Yeah," offered Warden.

"That's Big Mick. He could fire a 'sixty'[22] single handed. Blew the snot out of anythin' on two feet with that." Continuing in an excited voice, Ike identified the rest of his squad. "Guy on my left is Rankel. That guy could get laid in the middle of a firefight. We'd be out on a patrol somewhere and he'd just disappear. Pretty soon you'd see him comin' out of a hut with some local business girl and a big ol' smile on his face." Ike laughed – a pure, clear sound from his youth. "I mean, we could be in the middle of a frickin' mortar attack, and he'd find a way to get some."

Warden laughed too, thinking of the 538th's own Sergeant Mancuso, who had similar talents.

Ike was now leaning across the counter, twisting his squat body around so that he could look at the precious photo at the same angle as Warden. "Next guy's my best friend – 'Stash.' He could get anything we needed – booze, extra Willy Pete[23],… anything. Just tell him what ya' wanted and half an hour later he'd come strolling into the hooch with a big ol' grin on his face, carryin' whatever it was."

"Who's the guy on the end?" Warden asked, now fully engaged in the conversation.

"That's Washington. He was from *Detroit*." The handsome African American face stared out at Warden. "I didn't like him much at first – always playin' *that* music – but we became good friends there by the end. Stash and me used to kick the shit out of anyone who messed with him 'cause he was a Negro. Don't get me wrong – I'm no liberal or nuthin' – but Washington was one of the good ones; saved my ass quite a few times."

Warden nodded – things like the color of a man's skin weren't important when you were all just trying to stay alive. Ike continued to stare at the photo, hanging over the counter, breathing noisily as he rejoined his friends in their past.

"So, do you still stay in touch at all?" Warden asked, trying to break the silence.

"Humph?" Ike responded, straightening up and looking at Warden as if he'd never seen him before, as the smells and sounds of his base camp in the Mekong Delta faded away.

"Nah," he replied, sweeping the picture off of the counter with his right hand. "They...didn't make it."

A chill swept over Warden. "All of 'em?" he asked in a low voice.

"Yeah, I, uh, got myself on the first sergeant's shit list over sumthin' or the other, and he put me on an extra shift out on the perimeter. It was just one round... one...perfectly... aimed ...round. I heard the "chuff" of the tube out 'long the tree line in the dark and the whistle of the mortar round as it came in. It landed perfectly in the middle of our hooch – like it had been planned that way. Nobody told me 'til I came in the next mornin'. They never knew what hit 'em. By the time I came in, they had already tagged and bagged 'em. Everything...everybody was gone."

Warden knew there was nothing to say. Ike was looking down into the picture, pain traversing his face. Warden could see the young soldier now, still there behind the dirty apron and T shirt – beneath the middle-age spread. The eyes were still those of a soldier.

"I should've been with 'em," Ike confessed in a thick voice. "Maybe I could've done somethin'."

Warden said nothing. Ike wasn't really talking to him; this had become a one-man conversation.

"I,... I never got to say goodbye, ya' know? I mean, even after they were dead...I never got the chance. They were just gone...like they'd never existed." Tears welled in Ike's eyes, and the cigarette butt twitched nervously.

"They knew, Ike," Warden offered, feeling his own throat tightening. "They definitely knew."

"Yeah...yeah, I suppose so," Ike breathed heavily, as he slowly opened his wallet and placed the memory back into its proper place.

"Well, look who's here!" Monica's bright voice declared as she appeared from the back of the diner. Ike quickly hid the wallet beneath his apron as Warden looked her way, pasting a weak grin on his face. *She does look pale,* Warden observed, noting her gait was a little slower than usual.

"Is Ike takin' good care of you?" she asked in a dubious tone, noticing the spilled coffee in Warden's saucer.

"Yep, we're doin' just fine, Mon," Warden replied, watching Ike out of the corner of his eye. The young soldier had vanished, leaving the greasy short-order cook behind.

"I ain't got all day to be jabberin'," Ike said to the two of them, shoving his wallet away into his pocket. "Somebody's gotta' run the kitchen, ya' know."

"Thanks, Ike," replied Warden. "I 'preciate everythin'."

Ike caught Warden's eye for just a second, and the sergeant saw the young infantryman there again. Their eyes met in understanding, and then just as quickly the soldier was gone.

"Nnggh," Ike replied, turning and stomping back into his cave. "Gotta' clean the damn grease traps."

Warden lost track of the time while speaking to Ike and then Monica, so it was well after seven o'clock by the time his truck sped up the driveway off the county road. The Morrows had been there for some time, and Lil's look as he came in the door told him she did not appreciate flying solo once again.

"Hey Gus, how're ya' doin?" Bob Morrow asked, giving him a strong handshake as he entered the living room.

"I'm doin' good, Bob. How're you, Wendy?" Warden asked, stooping to give Mrs. Morrow a peck on the cheek.

"We honked at you in town today, Gus, but I don't think you saw us," Wendy greeted him.

"Really?" Warden replied absently, not recalling. "Where at?"

"You were goin' into that old diner over by the railroad tracks."

"Ohh," Warden replied, not sure where this was going, and reluctant to admit the existence of his refuge.

Lil arched her eyebrows. "Diner? Hope you're not too full?" she asked. The daggers in her eyes were full of accusation.

"I, uh, was lookin' for Jamie," Warden lied uncomfortably. He instantly hated himself for doing so. *Why am I lying?* he asked himself.

Lil knew instantly that this wasn't the truth. Gus was not an untruthful man by nature and on those rare occasions when he fibbed, he did so particularly poorly. His averted eyes and the blush on the side of his neck were dead giveaways.

"So, was he there?" she asked, refusing to let him off the hook.

"Umm, no," he answered, wishing that she would just drop the subject.

"What held you up? I was getting worried."

"Umm, I met this guy. He had been in 'Nam and was tellin' me 'bout it. I lost track of the time."

Lil could tell this was the truth, but was still bothered by the vibes she was getting from him. "Well, maybe I'll pin a note on you next time," she joked, trying to lighten the mood. Her husband's reaction was not what she expected.

Warden whirled on her, a snarl on his face. "Yeah, yeah, that's a good Goddamn idea," he lashed out, all of the suppressed emotion of that day venting itself at his wife. "I went halfway round the world and fought a Goddamn war, managin' to keep my men alive, but I need ya' to pin a note on me like an invalid. What the hell're you thinkin?"

Silence fell over the room. Bob and Wendy shifted uncomfortably. Neither had ever seen this side of Warden before.

"I didn't mean..." began Lil, embarrassed, trying to salvage the situation. She felt badly at having been so flippant, and hurt at her husband's overreaction.

"Bullshit... it's exactly what you meant," he spit. Turning back toward the Morrows, Warden apologized, "I'm sorry. I'm not very good company tonight." Giving a final steely look at Lil, he walked to their room and closed the door. As it clicked shut behind him, he thought, *I shouldn't have even bothered comin' home.*

Chapter 20
The Leak

Warden wandered into the cavernous storage area of the Reserve Center looking for Major Hirschman, the brigade's new Supply Officer. Colonel Hermann had appointed Hirschman to the S4 position as a parting "gift" to his successor, Colonel Burr, whom he despised. Known among both friends and enemies as "Major Attitude," Hirschman had been part of the "rebel underground," during the unit's Iraq tour, whose self-appointed mission was to frustrate the self-absorbed colonels from the 42nd, preferably on a daily basis.

Warden found Hirschman in a storage cage, inventorying equipment.

"Hey Sir, can I ask ya' somethin'?" Warden asked, stepping through the doorway.

"Sure, what can I do for you?" Hirschman replied good-naturedly, looking up from his work.

"I had requested some grenade simulators a couple months ago and wondered if they came in? I wanted to create some quick situational trainin' when we do the PT[24] test next drill."

"Oh, yeah, I remember that. Colonel Burr saw it on the training schedule and put the kibosh on it; he said we weren't gonna' have time due to your medal ceremony."

Warden looked blankly at Hirschman. "Sir, I'm not gettin' a medal."

"You are according to this, Sergeant Warden." Hirschman pulled a memo from his notebook and slid it across the top of a crate toward Warden. "Didn't The POD tell you?" he asked mischievously. "How unlike him."

Warden picked up the paper and glanced at the subject line: "Award Ceremony: Silver Star to Sergeant First Class Gus…"

BAM, BAM, BAM!

The door frame of Colonel Burr's office shook violently a half-second before Sergeant First Class Warden stormed into the room, his face dark and angry. Burr involuntarily recoiled in his chair. He had seen such a look only once before in his life: through the security peephole of a motel room in Montgomery, seconds before he crawled out a back window to avoid a potentially murderous confrontation with his companion's husband.

"Sir, I'm NOT acceptin' a medal for shootin' that Haji!" Warden declared, his voice echoing off of the metal filing cabinets to his right.

"Sergeant, calm down," Burr replied, trying to inject some authority into his shaky voice. The thought that Warden might harbor homicidal intentions had not fully left him.

"I *am* calm, Sir. I'm also damned unhappy. I'm not takin' any medal for *that*." Warden's cheeks were burning, and he could feel the initial pounding of an oncoming headache.

Seeking an advantage, Burr went on the offensive. "Is this how NCOs conduct themselves in the 538th, Sergeant?" he demanded, strength returning to his voice. "Stomping into their commander's office and declaring what they will and will not do?" He paused, hoping that he had not miscalculated. Warden might choose to use him as a piñata if he overplayed his hand. Eyeing the solid rancher before him, Burr had no doubt Warden could do so if he wished.

Warden hesitated. He knew Burr was a parasite, but he was the *commanding* parasite, and Warden *had* come on a bit strong. Smart NCOs learn early that they can get away with saying most anything short of treason so long as they don't raise their voice too much and hang a respectful "Sir" on the end of each sentence: *"I disagree, Sir; that's not the way to do it, Sir; maybe you should point that weapon away from the troops, Sir."* He chose his next words carefully, beginning with another old Army chestnut that really means exactly the opposite: "With all due respect…."

"With all due respect, *Sir*, I choose not to accept this award. What happened that day was nuthin' that justifies a medal – for valor or otherwise."

"You choose? *YOU* choose?" challenged Burr. "What makes you think *you* have a choice at this point, Sergeant? Do you realize that the Army Under-Secretary for Personnel and Manning is personally coming across the entire country to pin this medal on you? Do you understand that a dozen national newspapers are sending reporters to cover this?" The POD could see discomfort creeping in over Warden's anger and decided to press his advantage. "This is a historic moment for this unit and all of USACAPOC. Do you intend to disappoint this unit and all of its members by refusing this honor?" Burr's voice had now fully recovered, and he was employing every intonation and inflection trick he knew to convince the NCO to accept the inevitable.

Warden started to open his mouth, but hesitated. The POD's gambit to make him question his objection had been successful. *Shit, is he right? Am I being selfish?* Warden suddenly wasn't so sure of himself, and his head whirled with scattered thoughts and images: the Haji truck driver lying by the roadside in a puddle of his own blood; Connelly, the soldier who couldn't shoot because someone pencil whipped him through basic training; Jamie and his pathetic magnetic car ribbons.

As he searched for the answer, Warden's eyes fixed upon the Combat Action Badge (CAB) sewn above Burr's left breast pocket, and he knew. The finagling of the system by the 42nd's colonels to award themselves the "combat" badge for merely being in Kuwait during a missile attack – *that was thirty miles away* – early in the war had so devalued the decoration that it was now widely referred to throughout the branch as the "Civil Affairs Bullshit" badge.

"Sir, you've got a gift with words. I'm just an old rancher, and I ain't smart enough to disagree with a word you've said."

Burr relaxed with the confidence that he had triumphed once again.

"I can't reason it out like you," Warden continued. "But, I know what's wrong and what's not. This is wrong. The only disgrace I'll bring upon this unit is if I take somethin' that's not rightly mine. I can't do it, Sir."

Burr ground his teeth together in painful agitation. "You can't do it, Sergeant?" he snapped peevishly. "Well that's fine. I'll just pick up the phone and apologize to the Under-Secretary for disrupting his entire schedule to come out here, because some *sergeant* has an overly-developed sense of modesty. Then I'll call Major General Oldhaus and tell him it was all just a big joke: he's got a *helluva* sense of humor." Burr's voice shook with anger as he saw his grand plan falling apart. Standing, his voice reached maximum volume. "Then before,…*before* I toss my entire Goddamn career in the trash can, I'll invite General Merdier to bend me over a log for a few hours before he relieves me from command! Will that make you happy? Will that be enough to satisfy your humility, Sergeant?" Burr gasped for air as he finished his rant, his jaw jutting sharply towards Warden.

A light knock came at the door, and Master Sergeant Winkle stuck his head into the room. "Did you call for me, Sir?"

"NO! GET OUT, GET OUT, GET-THE-HELL-OUT!" the POD shrieked at the bland face squinting at him through his coke-bottle thick glasses.

"Excellent, Sir; I'll get right on it," the SGS replied quietly, closing the door.

At some point during Burr's tirade, Warden had slipped into a position of "parade rest," a habit from his early days as a private when being chewed out by superiors was a daily routine.

Burr lowered himself slowly back into his chair. The telltale squeak from the cheap springs reminded him how much was at stake. *I've got to get out of here,* he thought. *I deserve better than this…than these people.* He mentally ran through the arsenal of tools that usually worked for getting him what he wanted. *Shaming hasn't worked, and intimidation has failed. Playing to his sense of duty – nothing. What can I…?* And then there it was: it was so obvious he had almost overlooked it.

Taking a deep breath before proceeding, Burr began again in a calm, falsely concerned voice. "I am not sure I understand your objections, Sergeant; in fact, I'm deeply troubled. The only explanation I can deduce is that you believe you are undeserving of this award, am I correct?"

Warden answered directly. "Yes Sir, that's it."

"That you feel your actions in Iraq were not, shall we say, sufficiently *valorous*, so as to warrant the Silver Star, am I correct?"

Warden paused momentarily, seeing the POD's slit-like eyes flickering as he posed the question. "Yes, Sir, I...I do. It was a routine mission and some bad luck, and that's all."

"Hmm, I admire your honesty; I really do. But you see, your old friend Captain Smith has signed a statement...an *official* narrative for the award that claims your actions were...*appropriate* for the award of one of this nation's highest awards for valor in combat. He has in fact issued an *official* statement to that regard. Let me find it a moment...." Burr pulled open his top left desk drawer and feigned searching for the narrative, knowing that it was lying right on top.

"Ah, here it is. Let me see... 'Heroism under enemy action,'... mmhmm... 'ambush,' ... 'disregard for personal safety,' ... ok ... and you 'shooting the suicide bomber at the last moment, thereby saving Colonel Hermann's life.' Yes, it's all here over Captain Smith's signature," the POD finished lightly, enjoying Warden's obvious discomfort.

Suicide bomber? Where the hell did that *come from?* worried Warden. *The Cap'n never mentioned anything to me 'bout putting that in any report!*

"Now here's the really troubling thing, Sergeant, if you don't mind me sharing my thoughts," continued Burr in a patronizing tone. "I have heard different versions of what happened that day from a number of people. *None* of them have matched. Captain Smith himself has seemed a bit...*confused* at times about exactly what happened. But I have still put myself and my reputation on the line for him and you, believing that what he put in this *official* statement is true. I have risked my own credibility on your behalf. And now, at the last moment, I have you standing here, telling me that your actions are not at all *worthy* of the Silver Star, while Captain Smith's *official* account clearly says it is. This is very, very troubling…hmmm?" The POD feigned an expression of deep concern as he gazed at the statement before him.

Where is he going with thi… Warden wondered, as Burr spoke again.

"Are you aware what the penalty for a false official statement is under the Uniform Code of Military Justice, Sergeant?" Burr asked, as he closed the trap. "I'm sure your old boss Major Trevanathan would advise you that it is five years in the Disciplinary Barracks at Fort Leavenworth. I'm very concerned for Captain Smith, as I'm sure you are. You *are* concerned for him aren't you?" The POD left the question hanging in mid-air; watching it strip the last shreds of resistance out of the NCO in front of him.

Warden said nothing, feeling only dark hatred for Burr rising up inside. His hands involuntarily clenched behind his back.

"Tell you what," offered the POD nonchalantly, reaching for the phone receiver. "This is all beyond my simple understanding. Why don't I just call Colonel O'Reilly, the Staff Judge Advocate at the 42nd CACOM legal office, and run it all by him? I'm sure he'll be able to figure out if anyone has committed an infraction." Burr paused, his finger over the dial pad as he tilted his head and raised an eyebrow in Warden's direction.

"Sir, Cap'n Smith was just doin' what you told him to," Warden protested.

"*Really?* You know, I don't remember it that way – *at all*. Was he also doing his job in covering up the fact that your assistant armorer has been AWOL[25] from drill the past two months? PFC Jamie, I think it is? Yes, I have the sign-in roster right here: Jamie did not sign in, but Smith failed to report that to me. I think a good old-fashioned 15-6 investigation[26] will clear up all of Captain Smith's transgressions, don't you?" Burr began to dial.

"That…that…won't be necessary," Warden answered thickly.

"And why is that, Sergeant?" the POD asked, pausing his dialing momentarily.

"I've reconsidered my position, Sir. I'll accept the award," Warden replied flatly.

"And that's because?" the POD continued, enjoying this fish on the line.

"*Because*, Sir?"

"Because it's for the good of the unit, isn't that right?" instructed Burr.

"Yes, Sir."

"Say it."

"*Sir?*" Warden replied, feeling his temper growing again.

"You *still* seem unsure, Sergeant. I want to hear it from you, with no reservations whatsoever, before I put down this phone. In fact – Winkle!" Burr called. The ancient NCO timidly opened the door a crack, expecting to be told to get out yet again. "Come in here, Sergeant Winkle: Sergeant Warden has some good news he wants to share."

Winkle timidly entered the room, uncertain what he was supposed to do.

"Go ahead, Sergeant Warden," Burr goaded, savoring his control of the moment.

Through gritted teeth Warden replied like a schoolboy, "I've reconsidered and will accept the award, Sir."

"And that's because?" the POD continued to press.

"Because, it's in the best interest of the unit."

"*Sir,*" added Burr peevishly.

"Sir," Warden repeated.

"Outstanding," said Burr, setting down the phone. "Winkle?"

"Yes, Sir?" the master sergeant croaked.

"Get out."

Winkle slowly turned and shuffled out of the office, muttering under his breath.

"I was quite certain that you were merely having a case of nerves, Sergeant," the POD continued. "Now you've put my mind to rest on this issue. However, in case you have any last minute qualms on Saturday, I plan to leave a voicemail for Colonel O'Reilly anyway, asking him to call me next week. Whether I just ask him about the weather at Fort Rucker or discuss Smith's 'false statement' issue and the AWOL in some serious detail depends completely upon your cooperation. Do you understand?"

For the first time in his life Warden found himself seriously considering choking the life out of a superior officer. He imagined himself going across the desk at Burr's smug face and wrapping his fingers around the man's pasty throat. Before anyone could even possibly respond, he could easily liberate the unit from this viper. Instead, Warden brought his hands forward from behind his back and looked down at his moist palms. *Already enough blood on these,* he told himself.

"Yessir, I understand," Warden answered bitterly.

Chapter 21
The Cop

"Daddy?" Amy Warden called out from the front doorway. "There's a man on the phone for you."

"Who is it, darlin'?" her father replied, looking up from a half-finished oil change on his truck.

"I dunno'. He just said to say he saved your life in Viet Nam." She crinkled her nose.

Warden smiled at the obvious falsehood. *Leader – gotta' be*, he thought to himself. "OK, Amy, I'll be right there." Warden wiped his oily hands on a rag as he strode toward the house. *Wonder what's happenin' with Pete?* After the Jaguars had left Fort Bragg, Leader and Warden had talked a couple times on the phone, but it wasn't the same as their time in Iraq, where each of the NCOs knew what the other was thinking by a glance. That loss of comradery was one of the few things Warden missed from Iraq.

"Hello?" he said, picking up the phone on the kitchen counter.

"Is this Sergeant First Class Warden?" asked a familiar Philadelphia accent. "Hero of the Battle of Al Salaam and combat action figure?"

"Leader, when'd they start letting sex offenders out of prison again?" Warden replied.

"Warning! This call is from a federal correctional facility!" mimicked Leader into Warden's ear, affecting the nasal tone of a recorded phone message.

"What's up, amigo?" Warden began again, now that the expected preliminary banter was out of the way.

"I'm comin' down to see you this Friday," Leader began. "Give you the chance to buy me a beer."

"Umm, this weekend might not be so good, Pete. There's a thing at the Reserve Center I gotta' take care of. I can't get out of it."

"That sumthin' wouldn't have anything to do with a Silver Star, would it?"

"Shit, how'd you find out?" Warden asked in surprise, embarrassed that this fiasco had reached the ears of his wartime buddy.

"It's all over CAPOC, Gus. Somethin' like this doesn't fly below the radar for very long."

"Pete…" Warden began, feeling like a complete charlatan.

"What's he got on you, Gus? The POD catch you nailin' his wife or sumthin'?"

Warden was relieved that Leader realized this fraud was not his doing. "It's Cap'n Smith…and Jamie. If I don't go along with it, he's gonna' serve them up to the barracudas at the 42nd for givin' a false statement about the truck driver I shot, and for bein' AWOL."

"AWOL? Who? Jamie?"

"Yeah, his fiancée lit out on 'em; took all his money and ran up his credit cards, and he's been havin' trouble givin' a damn 'bout anything since."

"Lot of that goin' around," Pete Leader replied.

"Yeah, who else?"

"Well, not that I don't love you in deep and unspeakable ways, hombre, but one reason I'm free to come down for your award ceremony is I've kinda'…been suspended," Leader ended sheepishly.

"What happened?"

"Oh, the usual, espionage, running whiskey to the Indians; you know."

"What *really* happened?" Warden repeated.

Leader hesitated, but then began the story. "Well, since I got back they put me down workin' a beat on the docks."

"Patrol duty? With your experience, you're way past that, aren't you? Weren't ya' workin' undercover when we left?"

"Yeah, well, when we got back I was yesterday's news, and they claimed the only slot open was patrol, so they stuck me with some rookie and gave me the graveyard shift. I didn't mind really, 'cept the way they acted like they were doin' me a favor by givin' me my job back at all."

"The law says they gotta' do that, don't it? That's what Major T said."

"Yeah, well, they gotta' give you somethin', but they don't hafta' give ya' a big sloppy welcome home kiss or give ya' exactly the same job. You know the deal – Government's always the worst employer there is for bendin' the law."

"So, how'd ya' get suspended?"

"Well, we were doin' the drive-by checks down at Pier 5, and I noticed a broken window in one of the warehouse offices that hadn't been there the night before. We went to check it out, and some drug addict was in there robbin' the place; he squeezes off a couple shots at us and takes off runnin'. My rookie huddled down behind the unit crappin' hisself, so I took off after the guy on foot. This punk was runnin' and shootin' wildly behind himself; he couldn't have hit me if he tried. The guy was fast, though; I lost him for a second down near the cranes, until he knocked some pallets over behind a utility shed, and I found him hiding there. He didn't have the weapon on him and claimed he wasn't the guy who shot at me; claimed he hid there when the shooting started."

"That's it?"

"Well, not 'xactly. My blood was up pretty good, ya' know, what with him tryin' to kill me and all. That's somethin' I've always taken a dim view of. So when he wouldn't tell me where the weapon was, I bounced him off the shed a bit to encourage him to remember."

"And that got ya' suspended?"

"Well, here's the problem. He didn't respond to that friendly-like encouragement either, and so when my partner came 'round the corner I had the shit bird down on his knees with the barrel of my Glock between his lips, taking his 'statement.' The rookie kind of freaked and reported it, so I'm benched pending 'further investigation.'"

"Jesus, Pete."

"Gus, I know it was stupid. Honest, I don't know what the hell happened. I didn't even think about it, ya' know? It just seemed the most reasonable thing in the world at the time. I thought about some other scumbag finding that hidden piece and blowing away some kid or old lady, and that just wasn't gonna' happen on my watch."

"Pete, I'm sorry to hear that. I know you love your job."

"Well, I used to. Who the hell knows anymore? I do know that the punk started blubberin' 'bout where the pistol was the second he saw I wasn't foolin' around."

"So whaddya' do now?" Warden asked.

"I gotta' go before a review panel. The Lieutenant says I might have a chance at reinstatement if I get some help."

"What kinda' help?"

"Psych. They think I'm a walkin' case of PST,…PTSD, whatever they call combat fatigue these days; they want me to wrestle my inner demons and all that crap."

"Just 'cause you roughed up some punk that tried to shoot you? That's got to happen a lot on the force, doesn't it? I mean, when the adrenalin's goin' and all – can't be that unusual."

"Well,…sometimes…I mean you're right. It's not exactly department policy, but it's not unheard of either. Problem this time was when the rookie came round the corner I was…uh… apparently screamin' at the guy in Haji-nese to tell me where the weapon was. I don't even remember it, to tell ya' the truth, but that's what the rookie put in his statement. Scared the crap out of him – said I was yellin' in Arabic with my pistol jammed in that scumbag's pie hole."

Warden snorted at the image Leader painted. "Great, so you're gonna' drag your crazy butt down here now? Hell, I could probably get you made Chief of the Amarillo PD with that sorta' story."

Leader laughed. "Sorry, can't stomach grits. But I'm not missin' the chance to see you and the rest of the squad bef…, well, I just thought it'd be good to see you."

"Ok, well it'll be damn good to see ya', too. Plan on stayin' at the house, and we'll drive in to the goat rope together on Saturday.

"Roger; see ya' then."

Chapter 22
The Gospel

*S**lam!*

The diner's screen door sent a shock through Warden as it crashed into the frame inches behind his head. *Damn it!* he scolded himself for failing to remember the booby trap. A couple of truck drivers at the counter gave him a brief look before turning back to their meals. Monica was cleaning off a dirty table at the far end of the diner. She gave him a welcoming smile and nod as she loaded dirty coffee cups into the grey plastic bin in front of her.

Warden ambled down toward her and settled into the nearest clean booth. "Hey," he greeted her.

"Morning, hero," she replied with a cheerful expression.

Warden let the comment pass unanswered, wondering how he had suddenly earned this new moniker. *Guess she's just in a teasing mood.*

"Lunch or just coffee?" she asked, completing her wipe-down of the neighboring table top.

"Just coffee today," he replied, working a sliver out of his palm from the fence rails he had loaded that morning.

Monica went and returned with a mug. She sat down the coffee and then slapped down a half folded newspaper with a flourish. "Ta-daaa," she beamed: the headline announced "Local Vet to Receive Silver Star," above a picture of a much younger Sergeant Warden, taken when he had returned from Somalia some years before.

"Oh Christ...," Warden groaned. The first sentence was all he could stand to read: "Local rancher, Staff Sergeant Gus Warden, will be recognized with the award of the Silver Star for valor in a ceremony...." The rest of it blurred into obscurity. *They couldn't even get my rank right*, he noted sourly.

"Why didn't you tell me?" Monica gushed. "This is big stuff. I'm so proud of you!"

Warden blew out a deep breath, but said nothing.

"Or is it?" Monica hesitated, noting for the first time in her excitement that her favorite NCO was not even up to his normally dour self today.

Warden just shook his head, feeling increasingly trapped by the moment. *How had this all gotten so out of control? I just want to be left alone, and now I can either be a fraud or send two of my battle buddies off to the stockade. Beautiful.*

Monica looked down the aisle to see if her other two customers needed anything. Seeing that they were fully occupied with their food, she slipped into the seat across from Warden.

"Don't want the recognition, huh?" she started, wrinkling her nose in sympathetic alliance. "I understand how ya' feel," she volunteered helpfully. "Some fat colonel came through the amp ward at Walter Reed to give me my Purple Heart in front of a buncha' reporters, and I felt like a sideshow freak. 'Come see the AMAZING one-legged woman,'" she mimicked in poor imitation of a carnival barker's voice.

Her weak attempt at humor made just enough of a crack in Warden's defenses to elicit an appreciative grunt.

Raising his head and taking a deep breath, he looked into her eyes. They were filled with trust. *She's not gonna' be so trusting when she hears what I did. Well, I'm tired of pretendin'.* He gathered himself to shatter her image of him. "Mon, they're givin' me a medal for killin' an unarmed man who was in the wrong place at the wrong time. That's the truth of it. I ain't no damn hero. I shot a Haji civilian by accident."

Monica said nothing but leaned forward across the table, chin resting on folded hands, listening intently.

"It was our last mission – a week or so after Major T caught it outside Camp Babylon," Warden continued. "I was ridin' shotgun in the lead vehicle and thought we were bein' ambushed. Our convoy was cut off and this Goddamn Haji…this…," Warden choked on his words, "…he came runnin' out of a blind spot at me and the brigade commander's vehicle. I shot him down like it was the most natural thing in the world – didn't even hesitate. I can still see his legs turnin' to jelly when the round hit, and him collapsin' backwards, like in slow motion. I can see it all, right while I'm sittin' here with you. There goes his legs in two different directions; there's the crunchin' sound as his back smacks into the ground; there goes one of his shoes flyin' off. I got it all perfectly recorded – even though it's a little blurry – right up here," he tapped his left temple. "Only problem was, he didn't have a weapon, and he wasn't attackin' us. He was just some poor sumbitch' in the wrong damn place at the wrong damn time."

Monica's eyes stared intensely into Warden's. He waited for her rejection now that she knew he was a fraud.

"That makes two of you," she replied. Warden raised an eyebrow at the unexpected comment.

"Gus, you didn't cause that situation," she continued. "You were just in the wrong damn place at the wrong damn time."

Warden considered her words briefly before continuing. "I don't have any love for Haji's – not since Somalia," Warden admitted. "Never seen a buncha' people so hateful and self-destructive in my life. But that…," Warden struggled for words to convey his conflicted feelings, failing in the attempt.

"You said he was running at your vehicle. Shouldn't he have known better?" Monica suggested.

"Don't matter – he didn't deserve to die; he was just hurryin' – late for a delivery, maybe, and I cut him down with no warning. We tossed his body in the pickup truck like a sack of garbage and drove away so's we could all come home. We'd been away long enough; that was our excuse to each other. We'd earned the right to go home. Well, he's not goin' home – *ever*. Did he have a wife or kid? Do they even know what happened to him? His kin probably think he just ran out on 'em. Hell, I didn't even bother to find out his name. What does that tell ya'?"

"Gus, you were in a war, not a traffic accident. Your job was to get your commander and your men out of a volatile situation in one piece."

"But, I made the wrong choice and now that...*man*... is dead." The word "man" barely croaked out of the back of Warden's throat. It was much easier to accept shooting a "Haji."

Monica drew a deep breath before asking, "Did you? Did you really, Gus? Think about it: What was the right decision at that moment?"

"Not to pull the trigger. That's pretty obvious," he countered flatly.

"It's that clear, huh? Sittin' here in this safe little diner in Texas, it's all that clear? And was it that clear that day – a week after losing your major – with your commander's life in your hands? With your convoy just cut off? Was it?" she challenged, her voice taking on an edge.

215

"It don't matter. I screwed up, and he's dead."

"It *does* matter. What did you know when you pulled the trigger? What did you *really* believe to be the situation?" she persisted.

"I thought he was wearin' a bomb belt, but I was wrong."

"And why'd you think that? Did you just make it up?" Monica pressed.

"No!" Warden answered sharply, stung by the implication. "He was runnin' at the command vehicle; had this pissed off look on his face. I could tell he was holdin' sumthin' that looked like he was wired."

"And your team's lives depend on you. He's runnin' at your commander; he's not stopping; he's holding something. What's the right thing to do, Sergeant?"

"Shoot him!" he barked loudly, shocking himself with the certainty of his reply. The two truckers at the counter turned in unison as they caught this declaration, before slowly returning to their meals. "Shoot him," Warden whispered again, as an echo.

"Because if you hesitate…?"

"My commander and every man in my team dies," Warden stated matter-of-factly.

"That's right, Gus. Face it; you were in a no-win situation. You made the right choice – for the circumstances – the right choice for your men; for protecting your commander. The fact that it didn't work out the way you expected doesn't change any of that. Ya' don't get do-overs in Iraq."

"But, I was wrong," Warden muttered, clenching his fists.

"I'm not even sure what that means anymore, after Iraq." Monica offered. "You know better'n anyone that war doesn't give you clear-cut choices like in a movie. It's a constant barrage of no-win situations where kids and old people get caught in the middle and slaughtered, regardless of all the good intentions in the world. All you can do is use your experience and do what's right for your men. That's all you can ever do; where things end up is not under your control."

"Hmmphh," he replied, absorbing her words. At a deep level he knew she was right, but the desire to continue punishing himself was strong.

"Check, please," called one of the men at the counter, where the truck drivers had finished their meals and were preparing to get back on the road.

"Coming," Monica replied, as she slid out of the booth. She paused next to Warden as she passed. "You did the best you could in an insane environment. Don't beat yourself up forever for doin' your job."

"Even if'n you're right, it ain't no damn Silver Star moment," Warden replied, staring straight ahead.

"Let me take care of these customers," she replied. "I'll be right back."

As Monica rang the two drivers up, Warden analyzed his situation. *I'm stuck. No way out. I can't refuse the medal without sinkin' Jamie and the Cap'n, and I can't accept it without bein' a fraud the rest of my life.* Despair hung heavily about him, as principles he held sacred – taking care of one's troops and upholding one's honor as a soldier – were in direct and unavoidable conflict with each other.

Monica returned to the booth to find Warden still staring blankly ahead. As she sat down across from him, she offered, "Look, Gus, I know you're a good man and want to do what's right, but let me ask, what's the matter with just taking the medal to protect your friends and then just forget about it?"

"Believe me, I've thought of that and have tried to come to peace with the idea. It'd make a lot of things easier; but it just don't set right."

"But you…"

"Listen to me, hon," he interrupted. "Civilians see a chest full of ribbons and think 'Oh, what a brave soldier *that* guy must be.' Truth is the medals you get are for the real heroes who don't come back. When you wear somethin' like the Silver Star, you're wearin' it for those who died alone in some filthy hole during an artillery attack, begging God to survive. It's *never* your award. It's theirs; ya' only carry it for them. If I wear it without having earned it, it's like pissing on their sacrifice."

Warden paused. Monica waited silently while he gathered his thoughts.

"All those officers in our unit who trumped up badges and awards for themselves when we came home did exactly that," Warden explained. "Every time they put that uniform on with those bogus awards, they disgrace themselves and diminish the service of everyone else who ever wore the uniform. Now I gotta' be a rat bastard just like them, or two *real* soldiers go to jail and lose their careers."

"Seems to me your choice is pretty clear, then," Monica replied quietly.

Warden shot a questioning look at her, as none of this seemed even remotely clear to him.

"Sergeant, you don't get paid for goin' along or makin' things easy for people," Monica advised. "This whole mess in Iraq started because all the so-called leaders just went along with what was easy, rather than standin' up and admittin' that they didn't know what they were doin'. You get paid to lead and set the example. That's what my NCOs did for me over there, even when I hated it. You only need to decide whether taking that medal is in the best interest of your men or not. Once you answer that question, the decision is made."

"Hmmph."

"Now I got some dishes to square away," she announced and walked away to leave him with his thoughts.

Warden looked into his coffee cup for answers, weighing her words. *Crash!* The door behind him slammed noisily into its frame again as a deliveryman entered.

Warden's head crashed backward into the windshield. "Aambusshh," Mantis cried. Warden could almost direct the scene by now. He again saw the man sprinting from between the two trucks at him, a replay he had endured a thousand times since coming home. But this time Warden's vision was no longer blurred — he could clearly see the intense anger etched on the man's dusky features; he could clearly see the narrow object extending from the man's tight fist as he charged. No one else in the convoy was in position to react. With his peripheral vision he could sense the brigade commander clumsily struggling to free himself from his seat belt — his movement restricted by his bulky flak jacket. The Haji sees me, and he's not slowing down a bit, Warden calculated, as the distance to the man quickly closed. This isn't normal. He's a bomber.

Crack! Warden jumped, as the diner door again slammed hard behind the departing deliveryman. "They've really got to fix that damn door," he muttered to himself, mopping his coffee-stained lap with a handful of napkins.

Chapter 23
The Encore

After listening to Pete Leader and her husband trade war stories for several hours at the kitchen table, Lil Warden politely excused herself and turned in for the evening. At her husband's request, she was getting up early the next morning to take their daughter to her parents' house in Midland for a few days. Lil didn't fully understand why her husband didn't want her and Amy to attend the ceremony, but agreed that the sudden attention by the press was becoming disruptive. Two days earlier a reporter from Chicago had unwisely shown up at their ranch without invitation and had been escorted back to his car by a 2x4 toting Warden. The local talk radio was full of callers expressing their admiration for their local hero, and the need to "stay the course" in Iraq – though none of them were personally offering to actually help do that.

There had been several phone calls, however, and Lil had become adept at answering the usual clumsy probes for more information.

Warden had stopped answering the phone when it rang, but she had tried to be cooperative. Even Lil had to admit that many of the callers were clueless, with their inquiries of "Were you ever concerned for his safety?" or "Is there any risk of your husband being sent back?" She was always amazed that people didn't seem to realize the latter question was about as sensitive as asking a cancer survivor the likelihood of a relapse. On occasion, she considered replying "I'm sure he'll be sent back to his death any day now. Thanks for asking," but she knew that wouldn't help anyone, and the momentary satisfaction would give way to even more unwanted attention. She recognized that most people meant well, but just did not know what else to say about a situation to which they could not remotely relate.

"G'night, hon. G'night, Pete. Don't keep my husband up too late," she smiled, as she rested her hand on Warden's shoulder.

"I won't, Lil. G'night," Leader replied. Warden reached up and covered her hand with his, giving it a small squeeze.

After she had closed the door, Leader turned to his friend and asked, "So how're things between the two of you?"

"Alright, I guess," Warden replied unconvincingly. "Been a few problems," he answered more honestly.

"Yeah? Like what?"

"Well, I've been pretty tight since we got back. Lil's been on me to go see a counselor."

"Ha!" Leader laughed, momentarily irritating his friend, before explaining. "Yeah, I went to the VA after the wife got on my ass, too."

"Yeah?" asked Warden, interested. "How was it?" He was surprised that someone as self-assured as Leader had needed to talk to anyone, the one incident with the fleeing criminal notwithstanding.

"VA? Let me tell you about VA," Leader began. "I was home about six weeks when I had a bad run-in with my son. I've never put much stock in all that psychobabble; always felt it was just a crutch for the weak-minded, ya' know? But I 'bout took the head off my kid for throwin' a baseball toward the picture window of the house when he was pissed off 'bout sumthin'. I knew then I needed to get my shit squared away."

"What happened?"

"I don't remember if I ever told you this, but there was this Haji kid in Al Kut: He banged a big chunka' brick off the helmet of one of the Marines at the front gate while I was standin' there. I saw the little bastard throw it from behind a pile of rubble and then run, while that private went down like a sack of hammers. So, when my kid threw the ball toward the house it was just like that, ya' know? The arm motion – the angry look on his face? They all looked identical. I went after him like he was that Haji kid; I charged out the front door and knocked him on his backside. You should've seen the look on his face – terrified of me. Not good, man, definitely not good."

"Damn…" Warden murmured in a low voice. He remembered from their conversations late in the evening on Camp Babylon that Leader worshipped his son.

"So after that, I signed up to go see a shrink at the VA. Had to wait eight weeks for an appointment 'cause from the ten-second interview the receptionist did on the phone they could tell I wasn't 'dangerous or suicidal,'" Leader smirked. "Do a shot, Gus," he ordered, sliding a full shot glass of El Toro tequila across the table to Warden. Leader had picked up the bottle at the airport before driving his rental car out to the ranch.

"Nah, I'll stick to beer; thanks. Somethin' ugly always happens when I drink tequila."

"Uh-uh, you gotta' do a shot or I don't finish my story. Doctor's orders."

"Don't ever let anyone accuse you of bein' a good influence," Warden replied, dubiously eyeing the glass. Against his better judgment he tossed it back, and grimaced as he felt the burn travel down his throat.

"That's better," Leader continued. "So anyway, the day the appointment came around I didn't wanna' go, but I had promised the wife. I drove two hours to a VA hospital up in Pennsylvania 'cause Baltimore didn't have room, and then spent another half hour in the parking lot makin' excuses to myself why I didn't need to go in. 'I just need a vacation;' 'my reaction to the kid wasn't really that bad;' 'it will just wear off over time;' – all the excuses I could dig up. But somehow

I found myself getting' out of the car, and walkin' up to the building with the polite "Behavioral Health" sign out front that lets all the crazy bastards know where to go."

Warden laughed. "So, did it help?"

"You haven't heard the punch line yet, amigo."

"Go ahead."

"Well, I spent another half hour in the waiting room filling in circles on a form asking whether I had feelings of 'aggression' or 'paranoia' after a year with sixty million fanatical Haji bastards trying to kill me. Then the receptionist told me to report to room such-and-such, as the doctor was waiting to see me now."

"And?"

"Anndd...it's time for another shot," Leader declared, tossing back another dose of liquid fire. He refilled the small glass and pushed it over to Warden. Both NCOs were way beyond hesitating over the hygiene concerns of sharing the same glass. They had spent the better part of a year sucking out of the same canteen whenever their water supply ran low on a mission – which was *every* mission.

Warden sighed, recognizing "no" was not an option when Leader got rolling. He pounded the shot down, noting that it didn't taste quite so bad this time.

"So I walk down to room such-and-such, rap on the door, enter, and – this is no shit – am greeted by Doctor Abdullah, the VA head-shrinker for combat stress vets from Iraq," Leader laughed joyously. "I thought it was a Goddamn joke, ya' know? I half expected you to jump out from behind the door and yell, 'Gotcha!'" Leader leaned back on two legs of the chair, grinning.

"Let me get this straight," Warden replied unbelieving. "They have a Haji doctor doing the psych work for Iraq combat vets?"

"Absolutely! Nuthin' but the best for our boys," Leader smiled broadly, shaking his head.

"So what'd you do?"

"Well, I was a bit in shock, ya' know? I didn't know if it was a joke or a weird test of some sort, or *what*. Like having a Jap headshrinker for Pearl Harbor survivors; it made so little sense I was off balance. But it became pretty clear that it wasn't a joke after he began asking me all sorts of detailed questions 'bout my experience over there."

"What'd you tell him?"

"I told him....*drink*, drink, you bastard," Leader joked, shoving another full shot glass across the table to Warden.

"Pete, you're killin' me," Warden pleaded, but not convincingly.

"Drink!" Leader ordered, now fully in the bag. "What the hell're they gonna' do to ya' if youshowuptomorrowdrunk?" he slurred, "Send you to Iraq?"

Warden chuckled and downed the shot. He knew he was going to be hurting in the morning, but he hadn't felt this good since their last night at Fort Bragg, before everyone split up to go home.

"So, what'd you say to him?" Warden asked again.

"I didn't," Leader replied, becoming more serious. "I don't know what happened, but I started laughin'. Like one of those situations where you can't help it? Ya' know, when you're in a very serious situation and get the giggles, and the harder you try to stop the worse it gets? He seemed like an OK guy – for a Haji – but the more I laughed, the more serious he looked, peekin' over the top of his half-moon glasses with those big old brown Haji eyes, and that just set me off more. I had tears runnin' down my face, I was laughin' so hard; the whole thing was just so damned ridiculous."

"So how'd it end up?"

"After about two minutes of tryin' to stop laughin', my chest was hurtin', and I started thinkin' that if I couldn't get my crap together ASAP that he was probably gonna' call the boys in the white coats to take me away. So I just got up and walked out: left him sitting there." Leader paused, tossing back another shot, before continuing. "Nuthin' else I could do, really. I damn sure wasn't gonna' tell this guy that I see a threat from every Haji I meet now, and 'oh, by-the-way, do you mind if I kick your ass too?'" Leader's eyes welled with moisture as he rolled them toward the ceiling.

Warden remained silent, shocked that a "rock" like Leader had these adjustment problems. *I thought it was just me.*

"Yep, so that was my adventure with VA." Leader poured a new shot, but let it sit untouched in front of him this time.

"What'd ya' tell yer' wife?" Warden asked.

"Didn't have to. While I was drivin' home, someone from VA called the house to ask if there had been a problem, 'cause I had walked out. So, she was waitin' for me and gave me both barrels 'bout not tryin' hard enough, and not carin' what happened to our family. Said she was takin' the kid and goin' to her mom's house for awhile."

"Hmmm," Warden muttered. He could see the pain behind Leader's eyes for just a second until the NCO shook his head and once again pasted a defensive grin on his face.

"Yep, so that's pretty much when I made up my mind that I'm goin' back."

"Maybe that's a good idea, Pete. Hell, they gotta' have other doctors at the VA that ain't Hajis."

"Not *that* back; back to Iraq."

Warden felt a jolt up his spine. "Wh…Wha? he stammered. "Are you kiddin' me?"

"I can't cut it back here anymore, Gus. My life's a frickin' train wreck."

"Pete, we're all havin' trouble one way or 'nother…"

"Yeah? You shove a pistol through the front teeth of someone lately?"

"That was one incident…"

"Among several."

Warden was silent. *This has been a helluva' week,* he weighed.

"Look, Gus, I can't stay here anymore," explained Leader. "I can't turn it off. They said we'd take awhile to adjust when we got back, but I'm not adjustin'. I just keep replaying everything over and over again. I want to fight anyone who looks at me sideways and I jump like a scared puppy anytime there's a loud noise in my general area. I can't walk down the Goddamn street without checkin' the rooftops and windows for snipers. I live in suburbia for Crissakes! Biggest threat there is Mrs. Crotchrot, the old piano teacher, who eyeballs me when I'm out running. I can't help it anymore. My entire life feels like I'm stuck in those five seconds after the Major's HMMWV blew sky high. I'm always on edge, waitin' to get hit."

"Give it time…," Warden suggested lamely, wincing at how familiar and canned his advice sounded.

"I don't *have* time, Gus. I was in the grocery store with my wife last week when a lady next to me reached into her purse to answer her cell phone. I damn near reached over and grabbed her wrist 'cause she was movin' too fast, like she was goin' for a weapon. I was this close," he held his thumb and forefinger an inch apart. "If I can't tone it down, I may as well go back where those reactions are *useful*."

"Look, I know that seems to make sense now, but if ya' don't deal with this stuff now it's not gonna' get any better. What ya' gonna' do when ya' come home next time? It'll be the same…or worse."

"Maybe I won't have to worry 'bout that," Leader mused, before redirecting his reply. "I want things to work," he continued, his voice now husky. "I want them to be the way they were before with my wife and my son. But that's all gone. I'm ruinin' their lives; I'm ruinin' my life. I might as well go back where I understand the rules – where I can maybe help some young kid to not come home in a bag."

"Pete, you need to make peace with your family – not run away from 'em."

"Thanks Gus, but it's too late for me – for a lotta' guys. Young guys – nineteen, twenty years old already on their third combat tour? I'm wrapped too tight and I was only there a year. What about them when they finally come home for good? Only place where I fit in anymore is over there in the shit with them. I understand field-strippin' a SAW. I understand convoy operations. I don't understand the rules here. This isn't home anymore; that's home. I'm goin' home."

"Pete…"

Leader stood up, reached down, and popped back the last shot sitting before him. "One dead soldier," he observed, setting the glass down next to the now empty bottle. "See ya' at 0500," he announced, giving Warden a tight-lipped smile before turning and walking back to the guest room.

Chapter 24
The Reckoning

Warden bent over the sink, trying to shock life into his face with icy water. *How'd I let Pete talk me into tradin' tequila shots?* he asked himself. Dark circles under his eyes betrayed the cost of last night's reunion.

"Hey, war hero," Leader roared, sticking his head in the bathroom doorway. "Holy crap, Gus! You look like you were shot at and missed, and shit at and hit," he heckled joyously.

"Pete, turn down the volume, woudja'?" Warden begged, his head pounding. *I either gotta' stop drinkin' that crap or get a better brand,* he resolved. Leader was looking sharp in his dark green Class-A dress uniform. With a chest full of "thanks for showing up" ribbons he had received during the war, Leader looked like an Italian admiral. The single Bronze Star with its "V" device for valor at the top of his rack told the true story.

"You're outta' practice," Leader advised him. "You need to drink more, and you won't feel so bad the next day. Take it from an expert."

"That's great logic, thanks," Warden murmured, turning back to the mirror to fumble with his $2.99 black polyester Army tie. Completing a passable knot, he slipped on his own Class-A jacket, double-checking to make sure the shoulder tabs were not flapping loose.

Leader leaned against the door jamb, watching. "So how do you know Burr will hold up his end of the bargain?"

"Why wouldn't he?" Warden responded, checking himself in the mirror until satisfied his uniform was in order. "He gets what he wants; Jamie and Cap'n Smith are off the hook. Everyone wins."

"Yeah, that makes sense – from your side of it. But, what if he just keeps holdin' that over you forever – like a drug snitch. Those guys think if they rat someone out, they'll be off our radar screen forever. It doesn't work that way, though."

Ignoring Leader's comparison of his situation to that of a street snitch, Warden picked up his beret and looked at it with distaste. *This damn thing,* he thought, mirroring the opinion of soldiers everywhere who had to daily form, primp, and twist the unruly piece of fabric into proper shape whenever they went outside. *The old cover had been much more convenient,* recalled Warden – *and much less French. General Shinseki was a great leader, but a shitty tailor,* he thought, recalling the former Army Chief of Staff who had ordered the uniform change. Warden placed the cover on his head, twisting it about in a vain attempt to get the right shape and angle.

"Nice job, Pierre," Leader teased, as Warden scowled into the glass at his unsuccessful effort.

"Darn thing was jammed in my BDU jacket for a year while we were away and lost its shape," Warden complained.

"Here, let me square that away for you," Leader offered, plucking the hat from Warden's head. Leader turned it inside out, inspecting it with a practiced eye. "Well, Christ, here's the problem: you need to cut away about half this cardboard behind the facing or it's gonna' sit up there like a pastry chef's hat. Let me go fix this, so ya' look halfway like a soldier."

"Pete," Warden warned, "don't do anything too exotic. That's the only one I've got."

"Don't worry, I do this for all my guys up in the Baltimore detachment; haven't lost a patient yet," Leader grinned. "Scissors in the kitchen?" He disappeared for several minutes and returned with the piece of limp black felt. No immediate change was apparent, but when Warden looked inside he saw that his friend had carved away several inches of the supporting cardboard flashing, leaving a mess of tangled black threads.

Warden looked at the surgically altered beret dubiously. "Think ya' used enough dynamite there, Butch?" he lamented, stealing a line from one of his favorite movies.

"Relax; it's gonna' be fine. No one sees the inside when you've got it on. I'll clean up those loose threads afterwards." Leader stepped up to

Warden and positioned the cover on his friend's head, quickly molding it into "regulation" position: slightly angled, with the high peak of the crest centered over Warden's left eye. "There – that looks a helluva' lot better," he declared.

To his own amazement, Warden agreed. "Damn: you *are* good for somethin'," he observed, checking himself in the mirror. "I won't ever listen to your mother again."

"Ya' look good," Leader agreed with satisfaction. "Don't take it off, though, until I can clean it up a bit inside. You don't want any threads slipping out. Now, we better get movin'. I wanna' see the Sergeant Major before the ceremony."

Chapter 25
The Show

"Attention to orders!" began Captain Smith in a loud, clear voice in prelude to reading Warden's citation to the assembled guests and press. Smith stood behind a podium in his crisp, green Class-A uniform, ten yards in front of the parade ground bleachers. The audience of several hundred civilian guests sitting behind him slowly came to their feet. "The Silver Star is hereby awarded to…."

It's my job to look out for these guys, Warden affirmed, as he stood at the position of attention, uneasily watching Under-Secretary Brown fumble with the case containing the medal. *No time to let my personal feelins' get in the way.*

Without moving his head, Warden glanced at the smug expression on Burr's face, as Smith continued, "…demonstrated extraordinary heroism in the face of a determined terrorist attack…"

Burr was standing several feet in front of Warden, facing him from just behind the Under-Secretary's left shoulder. All three of them stood ten yards in front of Smith, Warden facing the audience. The unit was using the local high school football field as the "parade field." Captain Smith had arranged to borrow the grounds due to the extra seating capacity and because it made a better backdrop for the photos that would be in newspapers across the country.

The Under-Secretary finally managed to free the award from its case. The medal flashed brightly in the early morning sun, a silver five pointed star dangling beneath a white, red, and blue ribbon. Brown turned to hand the empty case back to the brigade commander. *I just need to put up with this for a few more minutes, and Jamie and the Cap'n are off the hook; the newbies will get the weapons trainin' they need, too,* Warden rationalized.

Warden glanced past the Under-Secretary, nervously wishing this was all over. He saw the press throng jockeying for position in front of the stands, twenty yards to Smith's right. The honor guard Warden had trained was an equal distance to Smith's left, their flags billowing in the light breeze. Several ancient members of the local VFW post huddled in the front row, wearing their distinctive envelope-style hats festooned with little badges.

"…without regard to his personal safety…" Smith continued.

Movement drew Warden's attention back to the right end of the stands where a photographer was trying to inch out onto the parade field for a better shot. He was quickly collared by Sergeant Major Woods, who conveyed with a single shake of his head that that was not going to happen. Warden sought other distractions – wishing he was elsewhere; not really doing this. A pretty girl in a white sun dress moved from behind the Sergeant Major, fumbling with a small camera.

It was Monica.

She had her hair down and obviously styled. Warden was surprised to see she was wearing lipstick, something he had never seen at the diner. Several of the old vets in the front row followed her with their eyes – the habits of their youth still well-ingrained.

The Under-Secretary stepped forward with a practiced, politician's smile, the medal held in front of him. Brown's perfectly styled black hair was sealed in place by an oily sheen, and a wave of aftershave assaulted Warden's nostrils as the bureaucrat stepped in close to pin the award on his chest. "Congratulations, Sergeant," he said and winked, as if they were two old buddies sharing a secret together.

"...placed himself in the direct line of a suicide bomber…" echoed Smith's voice from the loudspeakers.

Intent on working her new camera, Monica didn't notice the uneven ground in front of the bleachers until it was too late. Her prosthetic foot twisted in the soft earth, and the ill-fitting socket embracing her injured leg wrenched sideways, throwing her off balance. In an instant she was sprawled across the ground in front of the bleachers.

"Shit!" blurted Warden, losing his military bearing as she went down. Her fall also drew a collective gasp of surprise from the crowd in the stands. The Under-Secretary and Burr spun reflexively toward the disruption to see the young woman sprawled on her stomach, hair askew, and her dress riding up over a heavily scarred thigh and twisted leg.

Monica managed to pull her dress back down over her wound with dirt-caked hands, as she pulled herself to a sitting position. She knew at a glance that her prosthesis was broken at the ankle – her "foot" flopped uselessly back and forth at the end of the device. *I won't be walking on that again,* she thought, caught between anger and embarrassment. Pain throbbed from her good knee, on which she had landed hard. She was afraid to look up in the direction of the ceremony, but the silence screamed how much her mishap had disrupted the important moment. Her face burned with humiliation as she fought back tears. *God, why don't they just start again?*

A row of folding chairs had been set up next to the bleachers for the Army band detachment from Fort Sam Houston. Warden saw Leader appear out of nowhere and quickly carry one of the chairs over to Monica. He gently helped her up onto it.

Warden had lost all focus upon the Under-Secretary and Burr during Monica's fall. He could tell from Leader's face and gestures that Monica appeared to not be seriously hurt. Warden quickly recovered himself, as Burr wheeled back toward him, anger in his eyes and a dark flush to his skin. The POD started to say something, but caught himself and scrutinized the Under-Secretary to gauge his reaction before committing himself.

Realizing there was no serious disruption, Under-Secretary Brown turned back toward Warden with a strained smile. "You startled me there for a minute, Sergeant," he joked lightly, trying to cover his own nervousness. "Everything looks OK, though. That isn't your wife is it?" he asked with feigned concern.

"No Sir. She's a soldier," Warden replied, watching Monica over the Under-Secretary's shoulder, as she waved off further assistance.

Warden felt sick. Everything about this was wrong. Everything he had justified to himself about why he needed to go along with this was a lie. And now his own lack of courage had caused Monica to be publicly humiliated, he realized with shame.

"Really?" the Under-Secretary snickered in quiet reply. "They build them prettier than when I was in."

Warden resisted the impulse to choke the politician's scrawny, turkey-like neck.

Captain Smith, having recovered as well, began to wrap up his reading of the lengthy citation, "...bringing great credit upon himself, the Civil Affairs branch, and...." The Under-Secretary again stepped forward to pin the medal.

You need to do what's right for your troops. That's your job. Monica's words from the day before returned to him. *Then you'll know what to do.*

"No, Sir," said Warden, shaking his head. Again the Under-Secretary hesitated, wondering if frequent interruptions were a normal part of medal ceremonies in Texas.

"Excuse me?" Brown asked, looking quickly over his shoulder at Burr for some clue as to what was happening.

"No, Sir, I'm not acceptin' this medal."

"Sergeant!" Burr hissed through gritted teeth, stepping quickly forward and placing his nose inches from that of the NCO. "Are you out of your *mind*?" Then, realizing he was in full view of the crowd and photographers behind him, he backed off to a less-confrontational distance. Hate filled his eyes.

"I didn't earn the medal. It would dishonor my men for me to accept it," the NCO stated firmly, maintaining his position of attention.

"Sergeant, I'm sure many brave soldiers such as you feel that way," oozed the Under-Secretary, suddenly deeply wishing he was back at his country club in Northern Virginia. "Now, there's a lot of people who came a long way to see this, so why don't we finish this up, and we can talk about it afterwards, huh?" His mouth was still smiling, but there was no amusement in his eyes. He reached up again to pin the medal to Warden's uniform.

"Sir, if'n ya' ever intend to use that hand again, please don't do that," Warden stated firmly. He looked directly into the Under-Secretary's eyes to convey his sincerity. The politician looked back into eyes that were as dark and sincere as the gates of hell. He flinched a half-step from the promise they conveyed. In fear and fury, he turned on Burr as the crowd behind began to murmur at the obvious confusion out on the parade field. "Burr, what kind of circus are you running here?" he demanded.

Burr fumbled for a reply. "Sir…," he whispered intensely, as his mouth went dry, "this man has always been a malcontent…"

"So naturally you recommended him for a Silver Star and dragged me out from Washington to give it to him?" spat the Under-Secretary.

"*Sir*…" whimpered Burr, but his bag of tricks was empty.

"When I get back to DC your career is over!" Brown snapped at Burr, then turned and stalked toward his limousine, the medal representing the POD's future promotion still locked firmly in his grasp.

All color drained from Burr's face, and his hands trembled. In his mind's eye he saw his promotion going up in flames; he knew the Under-Secretary would make good on his threat. "Captain Smith," he called over his shoulder, his voice cracking slightly, "Dismiss the troops." Turning back to Warden who was still fixed at the position of attention, he whispered in a voice as flat and cold as death, "We had a deal. You're a dead man. So are your little buddies." With a final glare, he spun on his heel and began walking quickly toward the parking lot.

"Dismissed!" came Smith's distant voice.

Warden looked past Burr's retreating figure to where Monica sat frozen in place, her hands folded in her lap, eyes downcast. Behind her and on both sides, the crowd spilled out of the stands in a wave, each person seemingly unable to leave the area quickly enough. The press had chased after the Under-Secretary, who was only steps away from the safety of his waiting limo.

Maybe if I don't move, everyone will just forget I'm here, Monica fantasized. She was blessed not to be able to see herself at this moment: two dark streaks of mascara ran down her face, and the torn hem of her dress was stuck to her one bloody knee. She stared at the grass in front of her. *I've ruined everything. I disrupted the entire ceremony — that man even stormed out. Oh-my-God.* She wanted to turn and flee with the rest of the crowd, but she couldn't move. *I'll just sit here until the buzzards come,* she resolved, without humor in the thought.

Two feet in shiny black Army dress shoes appeared directly before her. She fixed her gaze upon them, refusing to look up, wishing them to go away. *Please, no…*

"Ya' know…," began a familiar gravelly voice.

"Please…Please, just go away. I'm *so* sorry…" she began before the words choked her.

"I'll go after I have my say," Warden insisted, using his *sergeant* tone of voice.

Monica nodded, keeping her eyes fixed on the shiny toes. A large tear dangled from the tip of her nose.

Warden began again. "Ya' know,… there was only one soldier on the parade field today…, and she had her skirt hiked halfway up over her backside." A shiver ran though her. *What was he saying?*

"There were others in uniform," he continued dryly, "but they were either bein' dishonest or lookin' out for themselves. Not bein' soldiers. Not doin' their duty. You were the only one who deserved to be on this field of honor."

She slowly raised her eyes to the deep set lines at the corner of his mouth and watched the words come.

"I want to thank you for bein' here to help set me straight. For everything. I haven't been actin' very much like myself for awhile now, and I almost lost myself. Ya' helped me get that back. Ya' helped me remember that there's no honor in compromising my beliefs – that I'd be disgracin' my men by doing what's convenient for everyone."

She raised her eyes and met his appreciative gaze. "I feel so bad…" she began.

"I would too, if I'd just mooned the entire VIP section," he replied warmly, humor tugging at his voice.

Monica bleated a moist laugh in reply, and felt her tears really began to flow, this time from relief.

"Look – ya' didn't ruin anything," Warden consoled. "This entire event was a cluster from the get-go. I refused the award 'cause it was a lie. I needed to let my men know that they can count on me tellin' them the truth – whether or not it's convenient. If they can't trust me, we got nuthin' when things get bad."

"Won't you get in trouble?" she asked.

"Yep, that's for sure. I'm done. Burr's gonna' hammer me for disrespect and whatever other infractions he can drum up. He's gonna' go after Smith and Jamie, too. But that's OK; I can live with that now. I couldn't live with it the other way. Just took me awhile to realize that."

Leader edged up to the two of them. "So, umm, when does the second act start?" he joked.

"In Burr's office in about five minutes," Warden replied flatly. "Pete, can you get the Sergeant Major to task someone to take Miss Gonzales home?"

"Sure thing, Gus. Ma'am, if you'll just wait here a moment, I'll be right back."

"I'm not going anywhere, Sergeant," she replied sadly, raising her wounded leg and watching the artificial foot spin freely. "Thanks."

Chapter 26
The Negotiator

The POD paced rapidly from one end of his office to the other, his stomach churning. *There's got to be a way out of this. Think. Think! You've been in worse situations.* Burr had not, in fact, been in worse situations, but it helped calm him to believe so.

I'll claim that it was a set up. I'll get a couple of slackers that I have something on to sign statements that they heard them planning this. Burr weighed the pros and cons in his mind. *But what if they turn on me too, like Warden? No…no, I need to keep this contained.*

He paced two lengths of the room before inspiration hit him. *A psych evaluation! That's it. I can't be held responsible if he's crazy, can I? I'll ship him over to San Antonio and get him certified as unfit for duty. That'll work!*

Burr stepped to his office door and pulled it open to summon Winkle. Burr flinched as he came face to face with Warden, whose large frame filled the doorway, his fist raised to knock. "*Warden!*" he choked. Burr moved quickly to place the desk between the NCO and himself. "Get in here!" he ordered over his shoulder as he retreated.

"Sergeant," he began slowly, once again beginning to spin one of his complex webs. "I'm afraid your behavior has become…erratic. I've been concerned about you for some time; I've mentioned it to several other people who agree with my assessment. I'm afraid today's events confirm my worst fears about your lack of emotional stability. I believe your unpredictable conduct presents a serious risk to this unit, and accordingly, you are hereby relieved of your duties."

"It's not gonna' work, Sir," Warden replied calmly. "Ya' can court-martial me, and ya' can fire me, but you're not gonna' be able to sell that I'm mentally unfit for duty."

"We'll see about that, Sergeant. Such things are best left to the professionals to decide…those who have experience dealing with *extreme* cases such as your own. I have a longtime friend over at Fort Sam who I am sure will be able to *help* you."

"Too many people know the truth now, Sir. I know that you blackmailed Cap'n Smith into this whole award fiasco just to get yourself promoted. The Cap'n told Leader."

"Guilty as charged, Sergeant," Burr smirked. "But do you really think that the unsubstantiated claims of several combat-happy junior personnel are going to stand up against a brigade commander's word?"

Burr countered. "Go ahead and tell them that I forced you and Smith into this. So what? No one will believe you. It'll sound so outlandish that it'll only serve to confirm your own unfortunate mental problems. No, this hand isn't fully played out yet. Secretary Brown is upset now, but once I present competent medical proof of your previously undiagnosed mental illness, he'll come around, and I'll be off the hook."

Warden glared at the magnificence of Burr's conniving mind. He couldn't very well *refuse* an order to undergo a psych eval. And Warden knew that anybody who hadn't worked with Burr would write the NCO up as a delusional conspiracy theorist if he tried to explain how carefully Burr had crafted the entire situation. *How do manipulators like Burr always seem to win?* Warden thought with frustration.

As Warden and the POD glared at each other across the desk, Pete Leader's unannounced entrance into the room surprised them both. "Well, Sir; you may be right," Leader interrupted. "Leastways, you woulda' been if it'd been just Cap'n Smith, me, and Gus." Leader turned to Warden. "Gus, let me borrow that sorry-ass beret of yours, wouldja'?"

"Leader, get out of my office!" Burr warned, his face darkening.

Ignoring Burr's order, Leader calmly took the beret from Warden's hand and turned it inside out. He pushed his fingers into the space between the felt and cardboard bracing he had trimmed just that morning, and pulled out a small metal disk. "What's that?" Warden asked, confused.

Leader held the disk up so that Warden and Burr could see it clearly, and grinned. "It helps to have friends who work narcotics," he said. "They have a lot of neat little toys over there, and sometimes they'll share. Gus, you've been wired."

"Pete, are you *nuts*?" Warden blurted, turning to face his friend.

"Yeah, but we covered that last night," Leader replied. "Sergeant Winkle has an open intercom into this office; he loosened the power bulb on it when he took the job, so it would look to the Colonel like it wasn't working. He heard every word of this scheme as it developed, and told the Sergeant Major, and well,…here I am."

"Colonel," Leader continued, turning back to Burr, "You just admitted to a false official statement, blackmail, and a host of other actions along the 'conduct unbecoming' line of bad boy behavior. That'll get you tossed out of the service with no pension if you're lucky and maybe jail time if you're not."

Burr's face was pale as he fought for words. None came as he struggled desperately to recall exactly what he had just admitted out loud.

"Now, since you like to make *deals*, here's one," Leader continued. "You're gonna' retire. Right *now*. When that suit from Washington drops the axe on you, you take it like a man and walk away. You do that, and this information stays buried. You don't – or you go after any of the Jaguars – and this conversation goes to the Army IG[27] and to CID[28] – they can fight over who gets to pick your bones clean first."

"That...that's an illegal recording," Burr blurted. "You can be prosecuted for even making it," he accused, making one last attempt to get the high ground.

"What're ya' gonna' do, Sir...send me to Iraq?" Leader clucked his tongue and shook his head, still smiling. "You can't blackmail someone who has nuthin' left to lose."

"Sergeant Leader – Sergeant Warden, let's all just calm down and work this out, shall we?" Burr offered, quickly changing his tone. "We can all benefit if we just pull together. What do you say? I'm about to be promoted, and you can both name your slots on my staff. Promotions even..."

The POD was still weaving a new scheme when the two NCOs turned without a word and walked out.

Chapter 27
Taps

Three months after the medal ceremony debacle, normalcy had returned to the unit. The new 538th brigade commander seemed fairly competent – as most officers go – having just directed civil-military operations in Afghanistan during the previous eighteen months. His focus seemed to be upon getting the troops combat-ready for their next trip to the box. "He'll do," had been the Sergeant Major's high praise for his potential.

Colonel Burr's death had been described in the Amarillo Globe News as "untimely." Leader had dryly observed in his farewell call from the Fort Bragg mobilization station that a nine millimeter round through the roof of the mouth is often "untimely." Unable to handle the humiliation of relief from command and his promised star being snatched away, Burr had ended his life the same cowardly way he had lived it – taking a shortcut.

Despite the VA's poor handling of Leader, they did alright by Monica, whose state of the art, computer chip-driven leg replaced her ill-fitting one. She had saved enough money at the diner, combined with her disability and GI Bill benefits to re-enroll in her hygienist program at the community college. She met another "amp" patient at the VA hospital – a sailor – who she was now seeing. "We figured we could save on socks," she laughed, introducing the young man to Warden at the diner one cold Sunday in January.

She didn't tease Warden at all when he had appeared with a toolbox that same morning and replaced the air cylinder on the screen door of the diner so that it now closed gradually and quietly. "Good job," was all she said, placing a warm dish of apple-rhubarb cobbler in front of him.

"There's no cobbler in Shitheadistan," she reminded him, when he tried to decline.

Warden was relieved that Monica now had some positive things in her life, considering all the support she had given him. Driving home from the diner he felt an uncomfortable twinge when he thought about the young man now dating Monica. *Seems like a decent kid, but…* Warden frowned, wondering whether his hesitation could be jealousy. *Nah,* he realized, thinking it through completely. *It's just because he's a Goddamn squid,* he laughed to himself. *I guess Marines gotta' come from somewhere.*

Warden walked into the house, remembering to slowly close that door as well. He found Lil in the kitchen conducting some massive cooking operation on the stove, involving several competing pots that were noisily hissing and sputtering.

Lil looked up expectantly, noticing his face looked a little more relaxed these days. He reached into his coat pocket and produced a letter-sized envelope, handing it over to her without comment.

"What's this?" she asked nervously, wiping her hands on her apron before flipping it over. Seeing the return address, "Human Resources Command, St. Louis, MO," dropped a heavy weight on her chest. She looked up at Warden, concerned. His face was unreadable.

"Open it," he told her.

Lil Warden pursed her lips as she opened the flap on the envelope and removed the letter with trembling hands. "Gus, if you're being deployed again….," she warned, her voice shaking slightly. As a career Army wife, she knew that very few positive things come from the Army Reserve's personnel headquarters in St. Louis – at least from her perspective. Gus wasn't up for promotion, so it could only mean reassignment, and most likely another overseas deployment.

Unfolding the letter, she silently read –

"MEMORANDUM FOR SFC Augustus Warden, 538th CA BDE

SUBJECT: Assignment to Retired Reserve

1. Pursuant to your request, you are hereby reassigned to the U.S. Army Retired Reserve, effective…."

She looked up at Warden's impassive face. "I don't understand…," she began, tears welling in her eyes.

"It's time," he replied evenly, stepping forward to take her hand in his. "I've been thinkin' 'bout this for some time now. It's time to go."

"But your men…, the war…?"

Warden breathed deeply before speaking. "Lil, I've spent most of my adult life trainin' to take care of others and puttin' the mission first – that's how it should be – how its gotta' be when you wear the uniform. But it's no good anymore – not for me. This mission…this war…it isn't gonna' end; it's just gonna' keep on goin'. Afghanistan and Iraq – they were just the start. Most folks don't know we're still just in the top of the first inning. Iran, someday Pakistan, and Saudi – it's all gonna' blow. And that's a reason to stay – to make a difference when it happens. It's why I've been spendin' all that extra time at the unit tryin' to get the newbies up to standard for what's comin' next."

"So why this?" she asked, holding the letter in front of her.

"You and Amy…you've supported my career for long enough; sent me off to Somalia and then Iraq without a whimper. You were strong for me, even though you can't stand the Army – 'cause you knew it was important to me…and to my men."

Lil looked into his eyes, seeing the pain of memory there, as he reflected on all of the time he had spent deployed throughout their marriage.

"It was necessary, and I don't regret a minute of it – mostly – but I can't keep livin' in two worlds any more. I'm either in the war or I'm not. I can't have one foot in both worlds. I'm draggin' the war home every day – I wear it like a wet poncho. And on the flip side I find myself shadin' what I do with the unit by how it's gonna' affect you and Amy. I'm weighin' trainin' opportunities by how they might affect our family – by whether they'll result in me goin' back to the desert sooner – not by what's best for the unit. I used to be able to keep the two separate, but not anymore."

"Gus, I don't want you giving up your career for me," she replied. "It'll just make you unhappy and resentful. You're a good NCO – a good leader,...don't give that up just to satisfy me."

Warden nodded before speaking. "I know… that's what took me awhile to reach this decision. But then it came to me that I'm not givin' it up for you. I'm givin' it up for *us*."

"Gus…," she whispered hoarsely, tears streaming down her face.

"I'm at a fork in the road, Lil. I can't wear this uniform and not get back in the game. If I stay in, I'm goin' back. Got to – it's been eatin' at me since the second week I came home. There's too much at stake to sit in a drill hall playin' soldier when there's troops fightin' and dyin' over there every day. And I can't stand becomin' one of those who draw a check from Uncle Sugar and hope they never have to earn it. Pete Leader reached the same conclusion – only sooner. He had to go back – couldn't take it here – but I've got a choice."

"But he just got home…you *all* did. It's been less than a year…"

"Yeah, and in that year the mission's been goin' down the tubes over there – rookies on short tours repeatin' the same mistakes we did. Believin' the crap coming out of Washington, that'll get ya' killed – that there's gonna be democracy in Iraq if'n we hand out enough teddy bears and smother the Hajis with inspirational talk and Power Point slides; that they'll all join hands and sing 'Kumbayah' if we stick 'round long enough. *Experience* is what's gonna' make a difference; NCOs who know the way they think; officers who realize a Haji isn't just an American with a tan and an accent."

"Gus,…you sound more like a man ready to go back than one who's retiring."

"I know…and that's why I'm retiring."

Lil tilted her head, raising a questioning eyebrow at his fractured logic.

"A lot of this don't make sense; I know that," Warden replied to her look. "I've been tryin' to rationalize my way out of this ever since I got home – waitin' for the memories to fade away; for things to go back to normal by themselves – and have just been diggin' myself deeper. The war's soaked so deep into my flesh that it contaminates everythin' I try to do. I need to get it out of my life so we can move on as a family, Lil. Cold turkey. There's no other way. I know it's all backwards, but I wake up every mornin' thinkin' 'bout that mess over there and what I can do better next time...to do something different that might save somebody's life..."

The image of the Iraqi he had shot began forming in his mind – *a blurry image running at him* – but this time he successfully pushed it away, choosing not to let the past control him. "It's there when I'm stringin' wire, drivin' Amy to school, eatin' dinner – it's always there... and it's not fair...it's not fair to you or her. I've got to put it behind me."

Warden turned and stepped over to the porch door, looking across the arid plain stretching out to the county road. "I'm also thinkin', I may wander over to the VA and talk to somebody 'bout what's been goin' on lately – the memories and such. Waddya' think?" Warden probed off-handedly, as he watched a cold winter wind stir up the dust.

"Sounds like it might be worth looking into," Lil replied nonchalantly, as she returned to stirring the gravy in an old iron pot on her old stove. *Yes!* she cheered inwardly, careful not to show her relief.

"If they got some damn Haji doctor over there, though, I'm walkin right out again," he challenged.

"That's understandable," she agreed, replacing the lid on the pot.

"And I'm not talkin' 'bout my damn potty trainin' or bein' in love with my ma or any of that other crapola."

"Wouldn't expect you to," she replied evenly.

"Well, all right then," Warden declared to the prairie, having run out of conditions. "Guess I'll be goin' then."

"Gus?" she asked from directly behind him. He turned to look into her hopeful face. "Thank you," she offered.

He placed her two small hands in his own, looking down into her face. *She's a damn pretty woman,* Warden thought, realizing just how little he had bothered to notice that since the war.

"I guess I didn't want to admit I had any limits," he replied. "I thought I'd be a quitter if I retired; what took me this long to recognize was that I was quittin' on you and Amy all along by stayin'; by keepin' myself *over there* in my head and not givin' ya'll what ya' deserve – a full time father and husband."

Lil could no longer hold back the wave of emotion that was coursing through her. Failing to suppress a massive sob, she reached up and threw herself into her husband's arms, her own locked tightly behind his neck. The pots on the stove hissed in their neglect.

"Ya' know I'm still crazier than bat shit, right?" Warden added, holding her tightly. "This stuff ain't goin' away tomorrow."

"Gus, you volunteer to sleep in the dirt and go places where people want you dead for trying to help them. I've known you were crazy for years."

"Man's gotta' have a hobby."

"I love you," she breathed into his shoulder. "Welcome home, Sergeant."

ENDNOTES

[1] IED – Improvised Explosive Device

[2] Sitrep – Situation report

[3] CIF – Central Issue Facility; the building on an Army post where soldiers are issued and return their field gear, such as sleeping bags, shelter halves, helmets, and other operational equipment. Loss or negligent damage to an issued item often results in the soldier being required to pay for the equipment.

[4] D-cell – Detention cell; often at the military police (MP) station.

[5] RPG – Rocket Propelled Grenade

[6] BDU – Battle Dress Uniform; the woodland-pattern camouflage uniform worn by Army personnel from 1981 through 2008.

[7] Adjutant, aka 'Personnel Officer' or S1/G1

[8] National Command Authority (NCA) – The President of the United States and Secretary of Defense

[9] At the conclusion of service in a combat theater of operations, Army regulations permit troops to wear the unit patch of their wartime unit on the right shoulder of their uniform as a badge of distinction. This is known as a 'combat patch' within the ranks.

[10] USACAPOC (or CAPOC, sl.) – US Army Civil Affairs and Psychological Operations Command

[11] 'The Box' – Army slang for the area of combat operations.

[12] KIA – Killed in Action

[13] MRE – Meal Ready to Eat. An individually wrapped field ration; T-rations or 'T-rats' are trays of mass produced food such as spaghetti that can be quickly reheated in a field kitchen to serve a large number of troops.

¹⁴ 'The Mog' – Army slang for Mogadishu, Somalia.

¹⁵ DI – Drill Instructor

¹⁶ MSR – Main Supply Route

¹⁷ Fedayeen – Irregular Iraqi forces who engaged in hit-and-run tactics during the Coalition advance on   Baghdad.

¹⁸ CSH – Combat Surgical Hospital (pronounced "cash")

¹⁹ Special Forces, aka "Green Beret"

²⁰ 82nd Airborne Division

²¹ 'Charlie' – Vietcong; short for "Victor Charlie" or "VC" in military alphabetic code.

²² M60 "light" machine gun; it weighs approximately 23 pounds.

²³ 'Willy Pete' – Slang for white phosphorous, an incendiary weapon used in grenade form, among others.

²⁴ PT test – Physical Training test; a semi-annual test of strength and endurance consisting of push-ups, sit-ups, and a two mile run.

²⁵ AWOL – Absent Without Leave

²⁶ Army Regulation 15-6 provides the procedures for unit level investigations of potential misconduct.

²⁷ IG – Inspector General

²⁸ CID – Criminal Investigation Division

PA
NS
JF

Printed in the United States
208579BV00004B/4/P

9 780595 492862